HELLCAT BOOK 1

# NIGHTMARE HIGHWAY

## WILLIAM VITKA

A PERMUTED PRESS BOOK

ISBN: 978-1-68261-188-3
ISBN (eBook): 978-1-68261-189-0

Nightmare Highway
Hellcat Book One
© 2016 by William Vitka
All Rights Reserved

Cover art by Christian Bentulan

**PERMUTED**
PRESS

Permuted Press, LLC
permutedpress.com

Published in the United States of America

# 1.

Athena Kozielewski grunts. Fills her lungs with smoke. Exhales over the steering wheel. Over her tight leather gloves. Grumbles at the sight of a few dipshit-looking teenage boys.

She squints.

The Dead Weather's "Bone House" streams from her USB hard drive into the radio and through the speakers.

She pulls her personally customized Dodge Challenger SRT Hellcat plus bull-bar—matte black with red stripes, bars across the windows and a roll cage inside—into the overgrown parking lot of the Dairy Queen off Route 28 in Jersey.

Fat green weeds worm their way through the fractured asphalt. They're tall enough to reach the waists of three dipshit-looking teenage boys.

Nature's happy running wild without the thumb of humankind to press it back.

Fuck our cancerous asses regardless.

Her tires don't care about any of that. They crunch the weeds.

Come to a slow stop on the crumbling blacktop. *MICHELIN* logo on their black rubber sides.

The Hellcat's 6.2 liter supercharged V8 offers the air a full-throated sigh through its vented hood when she shuts the engine off. Like a dinosaur. A big heavy goddamn animal that'll shit your corpse out an hour after eating it.

Athena leans her head back. Listens to the music. Mutters a mantra to herself:

*I am strong. I am death. I am the absence of forgiveness. There is no poetry for me, for I am that. Strength. Death. The absence of forgiveness.*

She opens her door. Worn-in leather pants not squeaking but swishing as she rotates her hips and steps out. Lifting her butt from the similarly well-worn Hellcat leather.

Cracked from the sun.

Tired.

Not falling apart but wanting to.

Athena takes a final drag from her cigarette. Grimaces against the sun in her eyes. Sneers. Cuz the eye black at the top of her cheeks ain't doing enough. She drops her American Spirit. Crushes it under a black pig-nosed Double-H boot heel.

She glances over at the trio of dipshit teenagers ogling her.

And why wouldn't they?

She's in durable, skin-hugging leather. Clothing that'll last longer than she will. Five-foot-nine. Curvy and forty-four years old. Good Polish skin makes her look closer to thirty-five. Blonde hair cut short for efficiency. No muss. No fuss. No bullshit.

She's probably the closest thing these pukes've seen within fifteen miles of the Dairy Queen depot that's counted as... Well, worth fuckin.

Which doesn't mean they ain't fuckin other things.

But Athena's a weird amalgamation of toughness and attractiveness.

She hears one asshole whistle. That cat-call crap. She locks her car with the red key fob in her fingers. Then tucks it into her jacket pocket. She shouts to the trio of drop-jaw goofs: "Leather and tools in the trunk if you watch the Hellcat. But don't fuckin touch it."

Money doesn't matter anymore, but she's got things of value.

One of the cancer kids scratches his crotch. This vague area near his dick covered by tan dungarees. "We gotcha." Could be STDs. Could be anything. Doesn't matter much.

People in the wastes of the old world'll fuck anything with a pulse.

Sometimes, things without a pulse.

Way to deal with these idiots is always the same: Promise em something better than what they got. Idea being they'd wreck your shit for it, but you offer that same shit as payment.

Oversteps some of the potential violence.

At best, Athena'll give the cagey shits a wrench and some fuel. Then peel out before they can do any damage.

These guys, they were probably babies when the germs hit.

Just grew up in the aftermath.

All piss and vinegar and bluster.

Thinking they're wily. Clever.

Maybe they're totally aware that they've been given a death sentence. Only reason they survived the germs is the cancer ate the bug before it could kill em.

Athena heard someone with a degree once say the cancer "metastasized" the bacteria or virus or whatever it was.

She watches the dipshits. "Nobody touches the car, everybody wins."

The itchy kid in tan dungarees leans his ass against the Hellcat. Plays his fingers along the car's curves. "Momma, I said we gotcha. Nobody fucks with 'The Scorpions' around h—"

Athena draws her stainless steel Springfield Armory 1911 Mil-Spec in a flash. Puts a .45 round through the forehead of the wannabe-tough-guy talking. The slug caves his face in. Blows blood and brain and bone out the back of his head so hard it arches over the Dodge and splashes against the ground.

The kid's carcass drops. Pisses. Farts. Shits.

Athena looks at the other two who were following him. Both stunned and stupid.

She says: "Don't touch the car."

Then heads through the rundown Dairy Queen doors and brushes by a shotgun-toting bouncer and bellies up to the quiet bar.

Ain't no jukebox.

No revelry.

Athena sits on a rickety stool. Cocks an eye at the scattered, buzzing fluorescent lights powered by some unseen generator.

Nice thing about the world ending in a flash is there's still gas to go around. Some folks've preserved. Some still being made around the remains of America.

Commodities don't change all that much.

And we never did get around to making this an eco-haven.

The half dozen men slouching around the place in various states of inebriation don't bother talking to her. The risk-reward ratio is screwed. Pussy doesn't quite seem worth the bullet they're almost guaranteed to receive.

What with that display in the parking lot.

The guy behind the bar walks with a limp. He's middle-aged. Clad in a greasy white undershirt. His long brown hair bounces around his shoulders as he hobbles from the far end of the bar over to Athena. She catches a glimpse of a bloated, golf ball-sized tumor that sticks out from his throat.

He nods to her. Tries to show he ain't impressed.

Feeling's mutual.

Athena rolls up her left sleeve. Shows off the foot long black untreated melanoma stain under her forearm. Says, "Whiskey. Refuel."

Her voice is gruff. Scratchy. Like she hasn't opened her mouth for more than a few words in months. Maybe longer.

Which's true.

Ain't been a need to.

The bartender crosses his arms. "Yeah, okay. But what've you got for me?"

Athena reaches into her jacket.

She hears the shotgun guard tense behind her.

His hands tightening around the pump Remington. A *squeak* of flesh on the wooden stock and his boots *clomp* as they find better footing against the tiled floor.

Athena produces a small bundle of cloth. Places it on the counter.

The bartender eyeballs it. His gaze flits up to meet Athena's. Then he's back to staring at this weird package. He picks it up. Sniffs it. Blinks and arches his eyes at the shock smell of...sugary sweetness. He peels back the cloth. Finds a stack of five small chocolate chip cookies.

He squints at Athena. "Mother of fuck, are these fresh? Baked fresh?"

Athena nods.

The drunkards and derelicts take sudden notice.

*Now* they desperately want to approach the leather-clad road runner.

The bouncer stands at Athena's side. Leans over so far to smell the treats he's bowing.

The bartender yanks a cleaning rag from his pants pocket. Feverishly wipes an area of the bar top to Athena's right. Sets the cloth and cookie stack down. As though they're sacred relics.

Real cookies might as well be.

The bartender slaps the burly bouncer's hand away from his prize. Nimbly plucks one up between his fingers. And chews out the first bite.

The cookies are perfect. Soft. Under-baked just slightly so, so that they retain moisture.

Not a single crumb falls from the bartender's lips. He looks like he's about to cry. "How long? Jesus Christ, I don't know how long it's been."

The answer's about fifteen years. That'd be when the germ hit.

Athena grinds her teeth. Knocks on the bar top. Arches her eyebrows.

The bartender pulls himself away from euphoria. Apologizes in earnest. "I'm sorry, I'm sorry. Yeah." He turns away. Rummages through the shelves for whiskey. A *particular* whiskey, it seems.

He comes back with a clear, slender bottle. Unopened. Holds the trophy up. "Eagle Rare. Good, American bourbon whiskey." He pours her a double into a relatively clean tumbler. Then stares. Then remembers her fuel. Hefts a five gallon jerry can of gas onto the counter.

Athena grips the whiskey glass. Sniffs the amber liquid. Downs the double in one shot. Sucks her teeth as the amber liquid burns its way down her throat. She nods. Locks eyes with the bartender. "Y'know, Evan Williams woulda been just as good."

She stands. Kicks the bar stool away. Snatches the Eagle Rare from the bartender and stuffs it into her jacket. Waits to see if he or the bouncer will object. Picks up the gas can with her left hand.

The bartender shrugs. "All yours. Thank you for the, uh—" His eyes fall to the cookies. "You certainly figured out how to make yourself useful."

Athena checks the other patrons. Makes sure the drunkards and derelicts haven't formed any pathetic ideas.

She backs away toward the doors. Whiskey in her left hand. Right hovering always over the .45 on her hip.

The bartender takes a stab at an appeal. He points to her. "Someone like you... We get a lotta visitors here. For gas or booze or guns. Right?" He tries to laugh like they're pals. "You could do something great with that talent." He juts his chin in the direction of the front windows. Where everyone can see her Hellcat and the crumpled body and the two dipshit teenagers guarding it without standing anywhere close enough to be considered "touching." He says, "I mean, maybe you should think about setting up shop here with us."

Athena shakes her head. She pushes her ass against the doors.

She's half-out when the bartender shrieks, "Wait! What the fuck. You snub me? At least I can run this place. I mean... Why? What'd be wrong with this? A safe place away from the crazies and the mutants and all the other weird goddamn shit that's taken over? You'd rather deal with raiders and wraiths? Ever even *seen* a specter?" His face goes red. He screams after her. "Are we *that bad*, you fuckin bitch. You tease. You fuckin *whore*."

Athena slinks out. Pops a cigarette between her teeth. "We're all goddamn dead, and I got somewhere to be before I hit the ground." She waves off the two dipshit teens watching the Hellcat.

They wait. Anxious for either payment or bullets.

She blows smoke. Digs another small stack of cookies from her jacket. Hands it to the nearest one.

Their eyes light up. Both motherfuckers are as appreciative as men who've been granted a pardon from death row.

The teens bow. Move away from Athena and her Hellcat. Happy to remain—briefly as it may be—among the living.

They maintain their reverence.

Athena clicks her key fob. Opens the trunk. Tucks the gas can in. Slams it shut. Opens the driver side door. Doesn't get in. Reaches for side-by-side sawed-off on the passenger seat. An old twelve gauge coach gun with a sling. Trades it for the full bottle of Eagle Rare. Lays the scattergun on the roof of the Hellcat.

Sure enough, the goddamn bouncer marches out.

Thinking she owes this place something.

Cookies or some other perversion the wastes force women to offer.

The bouncer barks. Holds his own shotgun up. Fires it once into the air. Pumps it. Like he's making a point. "We said we *wanted* you—"

Athena breathes smoke. Opens up with both barrels.

A storm of twelve-gauge pellets flay the bouncer's flesh. Most hit. Ricochet off bone. Pop back out the other side. Around his jaw. Till the kinetic energy of the pellets force the skin to come apart.

A few pop his eyeballs.

Rattle around his brain.

And the fucker drops.

Athena cracks open the coach gun. Pulls the spent shells from their homes in the barrels. Doesn't throw em away. Tosses em on the floor in front of the passenger seat.

She gets behind the wheel. Eyeballs the teens. Let's the Hellcat's 6.2 liter engine growl.

Athena gives herself a moment. Sighs.

First people she's interacted with since Edison and she killed two inside five minutes of meeting em.

She considers the ordeal for a moment.

Shrugs.

Not her fault they were dumb as bagged dogshit.

She turns the Hellcat back onto 28. Follows it north passed a dilapidated Wendy's. Jukes between dead cars with equally dead fuckin passengers.

When she sees car seats and tiny skeletal remains, she's mournfully happy she and David never had the chance to have a kid.

What kinda life would they've been offering anyway?

The thought depresses her.

She grits her teeth. Carries on. Hangs a left on Terrill. Right onto 22.

She bangs her steering wheel to the bassy drive of Deep Purple's "Smoke on the Water." In a while, she'll connect with Interstate-78. Then Interstate-80.

West. West. West she goes.

She'll hump I-80 all the way to California.

Through the wastes where America's maddening number of nuclear plants—a hundred and four of the goddamn things— makes itself known.

America was always power hungry. And the whole damn country had been on the better end of luck when it came to nuclear power.

Russia got fucked hard and fast.

So did Japan.

In America, well, we seemed to get most of it right.

Till everyone manning the plants died. Even then, most of the plants on the East Coast failed safe. The ones in the Midwest? Not so much. That whole third of the United States is having a fuckin fresh dust bowl moment. One with nuclear hot sauce and weirdos.

If luck's on her side, Athena'll see one of the land whales bored fuckers in bars talk about when she passes through.

Ah. Fuck it. None of this matters.

The only thing that does is getting to the Redwoods.

Seeing that sunrise.

Athena's gonna die. Some time or another. Just like every other "survivor" and for the same fucking *reason* as every other survivor.

The cancer she's got? The cancer that "metastasized" the germ before it could kill her in that fifty-hour window that killed off ninety-nine percent of America?

"Survival" is a joke.

There's no escaping the cancer.

Everyone around now, all they got is some extra time to be miserable.

To be a stumbling sad death.

But fuck that noise.

That self-pity.

Athena acknowledges her encroaching downfall.

She's aware of The End.

Tick tock. Tick fuckin tock.

All she wants is a sunrise with the redwoods.

And she'll kill anything that gets in the way of that.

# 2.

Athena opens up the Dodge's big V8 on the pathetic remains of I-78. Where the wrecks are reminders and the vegetation creeps over crippled dividing walls. Most of the brush is burnt back from other high-octane machines that run the Eastern Gauntlet for their own desperate reasons.

Athena bites her lip. Grins as the dots in the road separating lanes become a single, white-line. A nightmare of asphalt and paint. Black and white.

She's tempted to push the car as far as it can go.

Which's real fuckin far.

But that would mean another stop at another Dairy Queen for refuel. Or maybe a Friendly's.

Which could suck. And eat up ammo.

That last Dairy Queen scene was the best she'd seen for a while—and two people died.

Still... "Best" doesn't mean good. It's just a question of relation.

Relativity.

Athena eases off the gas. Pulls the Hellcat northwest along NJ-24. The bits and pieces of suburbia that surround her are strangled by green.

Sky a little overcast. Hints of blue behind the clouds.

And she breathes smoke.

And that feels just fine to her.

Which's a weird reminder...

Athena pulls to the side of the road. Near a red barn snuggled up against the highway. The whole place surrounded by fat bushes and vines that cling to a metal fence. The leaves seem unsure about what color they should be. Green? Red? Orange? Tan death? It's a mishmash of all.

She leaves the Hellcat to idle. Walks to the trunk. Pops it. Puts her hands on her hips and looks over her current cache of supplies.

A shitload of water treatment tablets—which plenty of sickies have threatened her life over. Jerky—some of it squirrel and cat and rat and dog, but still good enough. Has the calories.

Ammo for the .45 on her hip. Shotgun shells for the sawed-off in the passenger seat. Her scoped Remington 700 rifle and the .300 Winchester Magnum rounds to go with it.

Then flour. Sugar. Brown sugar. Baking soda. Vanilla extract. A one foot-by-one foot mini-fridge where she keeps what remains of her dwindling supply of eggs. Chocolate chips. Milk. Butter. Some dough from the last batch.

Then the prize: A goddamn Easy-Bake oven she routed into the Hellcat's electrical system. Modified by Athena, like everything else, so it can cook five normal cookies at a time on a straight sheet instead of the fun-size shit for midgets.

Athena opens the tiny icebox that's also tethered to the

electrical. Sniffs the dough. Still good. She doles out five mostly-equal dollops on a sheet she greases with Pam baking spray.

The timer on her fraud of an oven ain't worth dick. So she cranks the little Suzie fuckin Homemaker device to three-hundred fifty degrees and makes a mental note to stop again in twenty minutes or so and finish the small batch before the next rotten place she has to land at for resupply.

Athena closes the trunk. Walks back toward the front seat. She runs her fingers along the Hellcat. This ridiculous, gorgeous machine that's the only thing keeping her alive. Physically and figuratively.

She takes a drag from her cigarette.

Looks out at the once-golf course nearby that Mother Nature's having a fun time retaking.

Mother Nature apparent not only in the fat thatches of grass that grow strong and wild. But also in the hunting game. Mountain lions and bobcats that slink between green blades after the meaty reward of a deer.

There's more out here. She knows that.

Wildlife doing what it does.

Much as Athena does what she does.

Wildlife in the Radiated Zones is something else, though.

People tell stories. Lots and lots of stories.

Athena's heard it through snippets over the crank radio she no longer pays attention to. Bits of conversation between self-claimed road runners in bars and supply dumps.

Land whales, they say.

Insects the size of your vehicle, they say.

Weird, savage mutants, they say.

But fuck it all. Athena'll drive through it when she drives

through it. There's still better'n three thousand miles between her and her destination anyway.

This kinda maddening trip is gonna take *time* and *determination* and the readiness to do what needs doing.

Athena slips into the driver's seat. The Hellcat still happy on gas.

She reaches over. Plucks the bottle of Eagle Rare from its padded spot on the passenger seat. Lifts the whiskey to her lips. Enjoys a burning pull. Sneers as a flicker of David's face flashes across her mindscape.

Love.

She hates love now.

What was the phrase? "Better to have loved and lost than never to have loved at all?" It's ratfucking bullshit.

Tell that petulant, pedestrian, Hallmark Card crap to someone who was with a partner they loved for twenty-three years. Not *in spite* of the cancer they shared, but as a result of it. And then tear that partner away cuz of a goddamn raid by some profiteering scum in Perth Amboy.

And Athena knows it's not her fault.

But Athena despises the idea she coulda been quicker with her guns.

Not that she didn't make the bastards pay for every ounce of blood they took from David.

Every. Fuckin. Ounce.

She takes another pull from the bottle. Then another. Longer. Till it burns so bad she thinks she's gonna cough. Maybe puke a little.

Athena sniffs. Crams the slender whiskey bottle into a cup holder till she's sure it'll stay put.

She grips the steering wheel. Tighter and tighter. Till her knuckles turn white.

She snarls at the six lanes around her. Smokes. Pounds the buttons on the radio till she brings up a song she can murder someone by.

"Million Years" by Nico Vega fits.

At the first drum hit after the wind-up, Athena slams her foot down. The Hellcat roars for her.

She and her beast machine hit sixty in 3.6 seconds. Ninety follows soon after. Then one-twenty.

And it's fine. And Right. And Good. And True.

But Athena eases off the gas as she makes her way north onto I-287 all the same. Lets the car roll and slow to a more reasonable seventy. A solid cruising speed. Which's really just to ensure it doesn't hog so much fuel.

She's already gonna have too many stops on this trip. And she doesn't look forward to a damn one of em. Best to be economical in regards to gas consumption.

Maybe the Hellcat ain't the right choice for that. But fuck it. What she needs is power. Speed. Not some misguided environmentalist garbage.

Mother Nature continues her slow, unending reclamation. All in the form of lush greenery and the beasts that're more than happy to stalk the lands that are theirs once again. Coons and snakes and squirrels transform even the wreckage of the highways into habitats. Human homes are menageries—ecosystems all their own for the local flora and fauna.

Athena thinks, *This's all probably for the best.*

She watches two hawks soar overhead as the sun dips against the horizon. Both with wingspans of four or five feet. Mottled brown outer feathers and tan bellies. A mating pair. They dive after prey like fighter jets to her left. Near Lake Parsippany.

Her stomach grumbles. She's been on the road today for a few hours already. Maybe five. With not much more in her stomach other than a crummy "Southwestern Rice and Beans" MRE and whiskey. Plus she's gotta see how that Easy-Bake is doing.

So she parks on the shoulder. Takes another pull of booze. Shuts the Hellcat down. Steps out. Hits the trunk and peels open a Ziploc bag of dog jerky.

She munches dead meat while she checks the cookies and bags em.

Athena'd love to enjoy her food with a view of the lake, but that ain't gonna happen. This area of 287 is surrounded by crashwalls. Twenty foot concrete monsters meant to keep any chaos on the road *on* the road.

She sniffs. Crams a chunk of dry, cured meat into her mouth. Chews. Grinds the muscle with her molars. Thinks, *I need to flavor this shit better in the future. Maybe add some hot sauce. Cholula would be good. A slow burn.*

But there's only so much you can do with the stringy remains of someone's pet.

The husk of a foreign car waits on the other side of the median. Honda or Toyota by the shape.

A tiny, mewling voice chirps from that husk.

It's incessant and eager.

Demanding.

A tiny black-as-night kitten checks its footing against the lip of the open trunk. Meow. Meow. *Meow.*

The feral mother undoubtedly off on some hunting trip. At dusk, that makes some sense. Same as with the hawks. Better for predators with vision based off movement. Enough light to truly see. Enough darkness to stay hidden.

Athena reaches for a bottle of potable water. Twists the cap off. Drinks.

The kitten stares at her. Announces again that it wants *something*.

Meow.

The feline leaps to the blacktop. Sits on its haunches. Licks its paws. Stares again at Athena.

Meow.

*Meow.*

And in cat language that's effectively the same as: Who the fuck are you? Oh, you're one of those tall things. Gimme food and/or petting.

But the noise. The *noise*. The noise it keeps making makes Athena's ears perk up. And she quietly assumes the role of mother apparently never-meant-to-be.

She still has something very much like a heart in her chest.

Athena shoves another chunk of dogmeat into her mouth. Keeps one piece between her fingers. Lets the smell sink in. Doesn't bother pondering the irony.

She holds the food out with her left hand. Moves slow toward the kitten. Makes kissy sounds with her mouth.

The kitten maintains its mewling stance. Big amber eyes amid black fur. It watches Athena for fifteen. Twenty seconds. Ears bouncing every time she makes the kissy noise.

But when she vaults over the pale concrete median, the tiny mammal bolts.

And Athena watches it.

Tail in the air. Four legs pounding asphalt. Idiot. This black furry thing that could easily survive if it understood the nightmare world it'd been born into.

Which it can't.

And Athena knows that.

When those two hawks come back and tear the kitten to tiny kitten pieces covered in blood and brutality, Athena isn't shocked or surprised.

That's just the way of things.

Selah.

So Athena eats the rest of her beef jerky. Fills her stomach with meat and water to offset the effects of the whiskey she's gonna need more of.

She lights a cigarette.

Is there anything here she actually *needs* among the wreckage?

Scrap doesn't do her any good unless she has a forge and metalworks to operate from. In which case, she'd probably be focusing on mechanical repairs. She ran a diagnostic on the Hellcat's internals before she took off and the mad king-hell bitch of a beast is running clean. No current problems and no *hint* of a problem.

Except it's getting late. Athena doesn't wanna be on the road. Using her lights. Making both herself and the car bright targets in the darkness.

Athena opens the passenger side door. Reaches into the glove compartment. Retrieves a crinkly roadmap of Jersey. Same kind that started going outta style when the world got real spoiled on computers.

But, ho ho. Who's laughing now?

Well... Nobody. Nobody's laughing.

Most of em are dead.

Athena traces a path that takes her off I-287 and over to Lake Parsippany. She parks a hair's breadth from the edge of the water. In a concrete area covered by a sloped roof.

She gets out. Stretches. Listens to the waves in the cool breeze. Watches as crescent-shaped flashes of dying sunlight are captured by the surface of the ebbing lake.

Whiskey works its way down her throat. To her stomach and her bloodstream.

Nicotine does the same. Except by way of her lungs.

Athena hears three vehicles peel across the area to her east. Along the interstate. One big bastard diesel. Two V6s. Doesn't sound like the little engines are in pursuit—all three rides keep a steady throttle. So they're probably backup. Security.

Someone's on a supply run.

Much as things've gone fucked, there are still the highways.

Asphalt and engines.

Athena smirks.

Sucks booze.

Looks out to the horizon as the sad star in our solar system melts fully against it.

She mumbles. "Maybe this ain't so bad."

# 3.

It happens along I-80 the next afternoon. On a two lane blacktop somewhere south of Wilkes-Barre. In Pennsylvania's state game lands. Mean spot where the road curls west outta a northward straightaway.

An explosion. The squeal of metal grinding metal.

Athena slows the Hellcat. Rolls to the shoulder in neutral so the engine doesn't give anything away. But puts her in a spot where she can observe. About fifty yards away.

She puts binoculars to her eyes.

Sees how the rotten cocks set it up.

The raiders musta waited down the grassy green embankments on either side of I-80. Between the thick trees. Outta sight.

Way the wreckage is here. Husks on either side. It forces traffic into a single file through the turn.

Given the smoking remains of a white Ford SUV behemoth up ahead, it's easy to assume they set up an improvised explosive device that tagged the vehicle. Probably blew the front tires and suspension. Dirty bastards.

Athena takes personal offense to sneak-attacks against high-octane machinery.

It's all any mobile person has left.

She purses her lips. Ponders the scene.

Raiders fuck up the target vehicle. Swarm it. Rape or eat the people inside. Scavenge the remains.

Just good, solid fun.

Or, at least, backwoods Pennsylvania fun.

Desperation can turn us all into savage psychopaths.

Back when the banks still ruled us all, that savagery had different names.

Capitalism. The free market.

The raiders set upon the vehicle like frenzied ants. Rabid monsters. Ripping and tearing and ripping and tearing and ripping off the blue hoodie and jeans off a brunette woman maybe seven months pregnant.

Some man's body lies unmoving against the tar and rock of the highway. He's in jeans and a black and white plaid shirt.

The woman shrieks high hell.

And the four brutes playing their paws all over her, well, ain't been long enough for humanity to resort to spikes and football pads as their uniform or any of that shit. The raider dicks look like damn near everyone else.

They're clad in shabby clothes. Leather that'll last a while. Dungarees. Blue jeans.

Whole of America dresses like a murderous, grimy working class. There's no fashion anymore. No high heels or any of that crap. Just clothing that works and won't fall apart.

There is something weird about these bastards though. A mark on their foreheads. A demented version of the Ash Wednesday cross.

Athena locks the Hellcat. Stomps to the trunk. Grabs her Remington 700. Adjusts the scope and centers it on the skull of the raider who wants the first go at the pregnant woman.

He tosses the woman to the ground. Kicks her legs apart. Unzips his pants.

Athena's rifle cracks.

The raider's head jerks forward as the .300 WinMag round punches through the skin and bone at the back of his brainpan. Blows straight through the fucker's forehead and splashes the woman's screaming face with his gooey grey matter.

Athena yanks back the bolt. Clears the spent cartridge. Another takes its place. She snaps her aim to a second road raider. His face in slack-jawed confusion.

The next .300 bullet removes that face entirely. Creates a gory scalloped cave of red tissue.

Two raiders remain. They bark. Shout. Take cover behind the skeletons of automobiles. One of em screams: "Who the hell're you?" His form hidden behind the remains of a Hyundai. He blindly fires over the hood. His bullets never come anywhere near Athena.

She stays quiet. Shuffles partway down the embankment to her right. Goes prone. Steadies the Remington on the lip of the asphalt in front of her.

Then she waits. Silent. Patient.

Waits for one of the raiders to fuck up and poke his head out. To give her a target.

Doesn't take long.

The raider behind the Hyundai keeps his face tight to the

foreign plastic. Inches his head up. Up. Till his eyeballs come into view and he can survey.

Athena removes the top of his skull.

The raider's blood bursts up in a fountain that paints the car. One left.

The final fucker shouts more. Screams. He grunts. Some weird ape of a man. He crawls backward to the pregnant woman. She herself still too freaked out to do much more than moan and shriek.

Whole thing strikes Athena as a bit pathetic.

The raider jerks the pregnant woman up. He wraps a dirty, scarred hand around her belly. Places his pistol against the side of her head. Right at the temple. He shouts, "I'll kill the bitch. I swear to The Cross, I'll splatter her against the fuckin road."

Athena stands. Keeps the Remington up. Tucked against her shoulder. Her eyes never waver from her target in the scope.

She walks up the embankment. Marches at a steady pace. Slow. Determined. A machine. And she never says a damn thing.

She just thinks: *I am the absence of forgiveness.*

Which drives the raider nuts. He shouts more. Uses up his limited vocabulary. "What the fuck's wrong with you, huh? I said I'd kill the bitch." He shifts his weight from one foot to the other. Then back. His hand flexes over the pregnant woman's stomach. "You didn't hear me? Are you deaf? Mute or something?" There's a hint of panic. A shakiness in his declarations. "I'm gonna kill her. I swear. Unless you get the hell outta here. This doesn't have anything to do with you."

Athena stops when she's about fifteen yards away. Can't miss at this distance.

The raider starts to shout again.

A .300 WinMag round takes his gun hand off at the wrist. Carries through the meat. Takes a softball-sized chunk of flesh from the raider's shoulder.

He howls. Drops the brunette. Bleeds. Gushes red. Searches with his eyes for where his hand might've gone to.

Better to write that appendage off as a loss.

Athena slings her Remington. Pulls her .45. Marches forward again. Toward the howling raider and the whimpering, simpering pregnant woman.

The brunette grunts as she gets to her feet. One hand protecting her belly. She eyeballs Athena. Backs away a bit. Unsure about this fresh hell visiting her. She says, "Plea—" Stops. Collects herself. Says, "Thank you."

Athena cuts her a sideways glance. Steps up to the raider rolling around like a bloody animal.

He drags his shattered shoulder. His handless arm. The asphalt grinds against the wounds. Its coarseness taking bits of flesh as the raider mewls and crawls.

She says, "Any more traps along the road?"

The raider spits. Looks at her. Growls. Keeps crawling. He reaches his left hand up to grip some wreckage. Tries to pull himself up. Groans.

Athena puts a hole through his left hand.

The raider crashes back to the blacktop with a pitiful squeal. An Iron Cross made from small wrenches with a skull at the center dangles on a chain around his neck. The metal version of the tattooed mark on his brow.

Athena thinks: *Fuck me. I've heard about these assholes.*

Athena says: "Any more traps along the road?"

The raider whines. Stares at his ruined left hand. He begins to hyperventilate. Succumb to shock. He draws fast breaths through his nose after he manages to sit slumped against a car.

The pregnant woman finally snaps out of her stupor and scurries off to see to the unconscious man next to the white Ford SUV.

Athena stands over the raider. Growls. "You'll be dead soon. Bled out. On the road. Tell me if there are any more traps. I've got enough ammo to make sure these last seconds of yours are *real* unpleasant."

The raider licks his lips. Pulls em back to bare his teeth in a mocking smile. His eyes go wide.

Athena squats on her haunches. Puts the gun against his lower jaw at an angle. Fires. Knocks out all the bones and gum and teeth that used to be attached to the left side of his mandible. The bastard's tongue flops around in blood.

She says, "Nod or shake. Any more traps?"

The raider gurgles. His eyelids flutter.

Athena grunts. Blows his brains out. Stands. Struts past the other bodies and the pregnant woman and her unconscious ward. She heads down the embankment on the left. Scans the tree line for a spot that looks well worn—her operating under the assumption that these motherfuckers have been doing this for a while.

Nothing.

She does the same on the right side.

After a few minutes she finds what she's after. Beaten down grass and beaten back branches. Athena follows the trail. Thirty or forty feet into the woods, there's a ramshackle shack of corrugated metal and plywood. The grounds around the shitty little abode are strewn with prizes from previous kills and your general kinda raider bullshit.

There's a big black kettle that hangs over a campfire. The contents of which Athena has no particular curiosity about. Skulls on pikes—which must feel like mandatory accoutrements to whackos at the end of the world.

Ooh. Scary.

All Athena can think is: *It's been done.*

The only thing that stands out about the bones is the emblem painted on em: An Iron Cross made outta wrenches with a grinning skull at the center. Same as the dipshit who didn't wanna talk.

Athena mutters, "I get it. I get it."

But she's too far in now. She can't *unkill* the pricks. What's done is done. Whatever comes next is...unavoidable.

There are useless TVs and monitors and radios on blocks of wood. Some of the screens stacked and lined alongside each other to create a wide panorama of dead technology.

She keeps her gun up. Feels around the door frame of the shack for possible booby traps. Then kicks in the door. Checks her corners.

No threats. Inside to the right are four sleeping bags. All right next to one another. Which had to suck for whichever asshole raider was stuck at the end. There's also an empty walkie-talkie charging station attached to a hand crank. And a flag-sized version of the Iron Cross emblem.

To the left are two big cabinets and a workbench with various tools. Mostly simple ones—pliers, a hammer, some wrenches, screwdrivers. Athena reaches for two red bricks. The one on top with its packaging partially torn and a candy bar-sized bit missing.

Semtex.

A plastic explosive that's malleable enough to be shaped as needed. Used in commercial blasting and demolition—and loved by terrorists all over the world. Plus a remote detonator with a dial to determine which keyed explosive goes off when.

*This* she can use.

She tucks the Semtex into her jacket. The detonator. Opens up the cabinets. The first has a seemingly random assortment of ammunition. Lots of 9mm, which doesn't immediately help her, so she leaves it. She does grab a handful of twelve-gauge shotgun shells and a spool of detonating cord. The second has a strange assortment of knickknacks. Faded photos of...who knows. Who cares. A stack of map sheets catches her eye. The one on top shows this stretch of I-80. A circle drawn around the area where the trap went off. A square marking the location of the raider's camp.

Other sheets show more locations. Traps and camps. One or two west, along I-80. Some north and south on country roads.

Evil bastards have kept busy.

Also means there's a good possibility of *more* Iron Cross in the immediate area.

It dawns on Athena that some rotten raider ratfucker could be surveilling the scene right goddamn now. An idea buttressed by the sight of that empty walkie-talkie charging station.

Athena grabs the full stack of maps. The best find of the day. Then she heads back to the road.

The pregnant brunette is waiting for her. Some kinda expectation on her face. She says, "Thank you" again. Like maybe Athena didn't hear her before and she wants to keep that dialog going.

Athena doesn't acknowledge it. Doesn't respond in any way. She got what she came for. Now she's out. See ya. Please forget to write.

Miss Pregnant follows her. Keeps yapping. "We need help.

You saw what those assholes were gonna do to me once they knocked my brother out." She looks back to the unconscious man. But stays at Athena's heels. "If we could just get Mark into your car...get to the next town. That's all I ask. I'm begging you."

Athena struts to the Hellcat. Clicks the door open with her key fob. Places the Remington against the passenger side door inside. Slides behind the wheel. Slams the door after her. Sticks the stack of maps and the Semtex on the passenger seat.

The pregnant woman stands in front of the Dodge. Her eyes threaten a downpour. She brings her hands together over her heart. Keeps saying, "I'm begging you. Please. Just the next town. Please help us."

Athena grimaces. Starts the car. She reaches over the wheel and makes a swiping motion with her hand. *Get the fuck outta the way.*

Instead, the brunette pleads harder. Tears stream in rivulets down her cheeks. These pathetic wet trails. "I'm *begging.*"

Athena puts the Hellcat in drive. Lets the car roll forward. Hopes this brunette has enough sense to step away from the near forty-five hundred pound death machine.

She doesn't. She leans forward. Takes a Christ on the cross pose.

Then lays her hands down on the Hellcat's hood.

Athena stomps on the brakes. Shoves her vehicle into park. Throws open the driver side door and trains her Springfield Armory on the brunette. "Don't. Touch. The car."

The brunette jumps back. Hands in the air. Her eyes are wide at first. Then she locates her spine. And she furrows her brow at Athena. "You might as well shoot me. If you leave me here, more will come. And I'd rather be dead."

The pregnant woman probably ain't wrong.

Athena's ears perk up to the sound of an engine in the distance. One roaring this way from the east. Either a road runner like her, or some of the raider's pals coming along to see what's what.

She gestures with the pistol. Gets the pregnant woman to back up to the edge of the asphalt. Then gets back behind the wheel.

The whole time, the pregnant woman is shouting for help. Repeating herself. Getting more and more excited. Crying.

Athena moves the car forward. Once she's clear of the tunnel of wrecks, she'll gun it and outrun anyone else who's got ideas.

Then she hears the pregnant woman shout, "We can pay you."

And she bites her bottom lip and stops the Hellcat near the totaled SUV. Shuts off the engine. Grabs the Remington again. Gets out with a coiled length of plastic tubing.

She rushes to the Ford's gas tank. Notices an oval bumper sticker on the back: ADIRONDACK MOUNTAINS. These two are probably from some isolated little Podunk town populated by dopes who haven't had to fight in the real world.

Athena grunts. Sticks the tubing deep inside the Ford's gas tank. Carefully runs it back over to her Hellcat. Siphons the fuel into her own tank. Delays at least one stop for a while.

The pregnant woman waddles up to the SUV. Catches her breath. "What are you doing?"

Athena steps over the guy, Mark's, knocked-out body. She opens up one of the rear passenger doors. Starts to go through the supplies this brother-sister duo gathered before their ill-fated trip to...wherever.

There's a Mossberg shotgun. Shells. Could be useful. Not really *needed* though. What else? Lots of canned food. Again, potentially useful. The shit just weighs too much. She'll take the freeze-dried stuff, though. Ditto some toilet paper to replenish her own stock.

She doesn't care about the bottled water. And her medical supplies are better than theirs. But the baby formula and diapers are like gold. So's the Vaseline. Chapstick. And eggs. And powdered milk.

This Good Samaritan garbage might actually pay off.

Miss Pregnant sidles up beside Athena. Says, "What are you *doing*?"

Athena grunts. "Calculating your tab." She grabs the Mossberg. A box of shells. Moves em to the Hellcat's backseat. Tells the brunette: "Put the freeze-dried food, the baby formula, diapers, Vaseline, Chapstick, eggs, and powdered milk in my trunk." She nods toward the Mark guy. "What does your brother do?"

Translation: Is your brother useful?

The pregnant woman blinks for a moment. Two. Starts to transfer supplies. Talks while she does so. "He's a doctor."

Athena listens for that engine again. She casts her gaze east. Raises the Remington to her shoulder. Peers through the scope.

There's a tricked out mutant of a red Ford Mustang heading their way. Spoilers on the back. Barbed wire around the doors. Spikes jutting from the hub caps.

She doesn't look back to the brunette. Athena keeps her eyes in the scope. Says, "Your brother a real doctor or one of those bullshit 'doctors' like sociologists and philosophers."

Miss Pregnant huffs with exertion. She lifts the stacks of baby formula. "He's a real doctor. That's why he's with me. To help with the...the baby."

Athena watches the Ford. When it gets close enough, she sends a WinMag round through the window on the driver's side.

The bullet bulldozes through the glass. There's a nice splash inside. And the Mustang veers madly off the road. It flips. Crashes. Smashes into trees and comes to a stop upside down.

Athena slings the rifle. Gestures for the pregnant woman—who has a dumb look of awe on her face from the last spectacle—to keep moving supplies. Then says, "When you're done with that, I'll get your brother's shoulders. You get his feet."

# 4.

The pregnant woman has a problem with her mouth.

She never shuts it.

The pregnant woman looks around the Hellcat's black interior. Accents in upholstery and lights in red. She talks while she gawks. "My name is Michelle. When Mark wakes up—"

Athena grunts. "Dunno when that's gonna happen."

Michelle adjusts her ass in the passenger seat. "Why. What do you mean?" She turns to face Athena. Moves her seatbelt around her belly in an attempt to make it comfortable.

"Well—" Athena feigns a smile from behind the wheel.

Visions of David flash across her mindscape.

And she wants to say, *Lemme explain how concussions work. Lemme explain how trauma works. The sandpaper-like interior of your brother's skull is rubbing up against his brain in ways that're causing it to bleed and maybe he'll never wake up. I'm still dropping you off and keeping your stuff, by the way.*

Instead she lights a cigarette. Says, "Your brother took an intense beating. He's a doctor. I'm not. But you don't shake off that kinda thing. Could be another couple hours. Could be a day or more. And when he wakes up..." Athena shrugs.

Michelle tugs on her seatbelt. "Don't...shrug. Jesus. What're you saying?"

Athena blows smoke. "He could've suffered a stroke. Maybe an aneurysm. Wouldn't be the guy you knew before."

Michelle looks back at her brother. The corners of her lips drawn down. Eyes threaten that same kinda torrential downpour as when she was desperate for a ride.

Then she waves her hand in front of her face against Athena's cigarette smoke. "Do you mind? I'm pregnant for fuck's sake."

Athena snarls. Turns her head slow toward this mouthy Michelle in the passenger seat. "You're in my car, you senseless cunt. I'm the driver. There's no rule you can make that I need to obey."

Michelle frowns. "The smoke can hurt the baby."

Athena squints at Michelle. "How old are you?"

"Twenty-three." She shifts in the seat again.

Athena licks her lips. "The generation that stopped the goddamn Nazis grew up with a lot worse. But you're part of the pussy generation, huh? The *me me me*. Instant gratification and acknowledgement shit."

Michelle snorts. "You're what? In your late thirties?"

"Forty-four."

Michelle arches her eyebrows. "Forty-four. You coulda had me, y'know. This is a conversation you could be having with your own daughter, but you're being such an entitled bitch we'd never communicate. The *I suffered more than you did* thing."

Athena considers it. Tightens her grip around the steering wheel. "I'm still not putting out my stogie." Sniffs. "If you're twenty-three, how old is your brother? How's a guy like that become a doctor now?"

"Different moms." Michelle glances out the window. "He's closer to your age. Forty-two. Our dad liked setting up franchises across generations."

Athena smirks. Steers around a few wrecks. Says, "What's your end game here?"

Michelle rubs her belly. "My baby doesn't have the germ or the cancer." She looks through the Hellcat's windshield. "There's a place in California. A place the radio says is there. Where they're trying to start everything again."

Athena rolls her eyes. "Some kinda Eden."

Michelle nods. "That's what they say. Way north. Where the big trees are."

Athena sneers. Doesn't like the idea that *her* refuge for a quiet death is someone else's. "And the father. Where's he?"

"He, uh..." Michelle frowns. The reflections of greenery play against her face. "We were in the Catskills when everything happened. And, uh." She rubs her belly. "A man came into town. And he was a good man. And he did what he could for us. And he was strong. And..." She wipes her eyes. "And when too many of the raiders came, they surrounded him, and they forced him down, and they kicked his face into the curb."

Michelle nods. Lips tight. Eyes leaking. She's silent except the oncoming heaves of sorrow. "And now he doesn't exist. But I remember the sound. That horrible sound."

She tilts her head toward Athena.

And Athena nods.

And Athena says, "Yeah."

# 5.

They pull into Love's Travel Stop. After Athena's had her nicotine and booze and has successfully avoided the other traps the raider gang set up.

Much of which meant going off-road.

Which means the Hellcat needs a wash.

Athena pulls em into the big two-plus acre lot Love's sits on.

Cracked asphalt and rotting eighteen wheelers with their cargo long since attacked for scrap and bartering.

The way the place sits, just southeast of the Susquehanna River, it's a sprawl of blacktop and urgency. You stop there if you wanna eat and fuel up and maybe have a hope of surviving the next two hundred miles.

There are four main buildings. The southeastern one used to be a Subway with a Sunoco attached. Now there are hand painted signs that boast about a selection of guns and ammo. Across the street to the west are the remains of a two-story U-shaped Motel

6. The big lot there filled with hookers and their cancerous pimps. Going rate for pussy and a room is whatever can be bartered.

A McDonald's waits kitty-corner to the giant brothel. Obviously no longer a fast food haven. It apparently sells clothing now. The actual Love's is last. Waiting in the northwestern plot. It hasn't changed much in fifteen years. It's a refuge for food and fuel and booze and mechanical needs.

What Athena really *doesn't* like is the apparent fact that whoever's in charge here is also in charge of the bridge over the Susquehanna. She can see militia types guarding both the close-by southern entrance and the northern. When either the desperate or the powerful guard something they're sure is *theirs*, it makes the lives of everyone else a nightmare.

Athena stops the car in front of Love's. The Hellcat's not as much of a rarity among other road runners' rigs. But plenty of eyeballs play over her and her dirty vehicle all the same.

She glances at some of the other machines. A couple of kitted out Honda Accords with V6s that're hard to kill—even if you're an inept driver. Chevy Corvettes and Camaros. A Dodge Charger and Challenger. A sexy little 2004 Ford GT. A handful of Subaru Impreza WRXs. Some dirt bikes. Pickup trucks.

Nice thing about the world ending the way it did is everyone got or gets their pick of automobiles. There aren't any salesmen to get past. No loans to worry about. Payments. Find a metal machine you love and make sure you can keep it running.

Athena grins. Other than the vicious fuckers who *own* the vehicles, this's a scene she can get into. A lotta metal and leather. She tilts her head toward Michelle. Says, "I'm getting a drink. You're on your own from here on out."

Michelle blinks. She accidentally locks eyes with some of the meaner-looking bastards in the parking lot. Then snaps herself out of it and stares at Athena. "You can't leave us here. They'll tear us to pieces. Mark isn't even *awake* yet."

Doesn't matter.

Athena's outta the Hellcat. Keys in hand. She struts around to Michelle's side. Opens the door. Shoots the pregnant woman a look, then turns her eyes up to keep watch over the others in the lot. "Get out, mountain girl."

Michelle doesn't move. She looks confused. A frown on her face.

Athena says again: "Get the fuck outta the car."

Michelle shakes her head. "You can't leave us here."

Athena pulls her .45. Grunts. "I did *exactly* what I said I was gonna. It's called a verbal contract. And unlike some of the other shitlords out here, I didn't try to rape or eat you in the process." She fires a shot into the air. To make an impression on both Michelle and the audience. "Get the fuck outta the car."

The other road runners take a step back. Chuckle nervously.

Michelle snakes one leg out. Then another. Must've dawned on her that moving is a good idea. She stands beside the Hellcat. Sneers at Athena. "You're killing us." Her lips tremble.

Athena feigns a curt smile. Pushes Michelle outta the way. Farther along the blacktop. Reaches in to grab Mark.

His eyes flip open when she grabs his shoulders. His brow shoots down. There's recognition in his eyes. An awareness of the situation that Athena doesn't like. His mouth opens. Mark starts to say something.

Which doesn't matter one fuckin jot.

Athena drags him from the backseat. Not an easy task, since Mark's six-foot-two. But she lays him on the pavement. Locks the Hellcat. Marches toward Love's and the booze inside.

She leaves the small-town brother and sister to figure it out on their own.

Which they won't.

Which she knows.

Which she's trying to ignore.

* * *

Five seconds after Athena passes through Love's doors, one road running dipshit hits on her. Then another. And another.

Probably cuz her cancer doesn't look so bad. It doesn't blow up in ugly bulges. Leak. Press against the windpipe or the lungs.

And it strikes Athena that she's the best of a bad situation.

That in and of itself fuckin sucks.

That realization when you're thrumming along America's veins. When you're in America's organs. The highways and the weird truck stops and the vehicles that kept the country going.

The roads and the machines.

The monkeys of need.

Someone tickles Athena's left hand. Fat fingers play along her palm.

Athena turns and sees some Big Bertha type bitch smiling.

Athena smiles back.

Then rams the barrel of her .45 into Big Bertha's forehead. Once. Twice.

Till Big Bertha's forehead cracks and the lumpy bitch goes down.

The crowd backs off.

Athena bares her teeth. Pans her gaze from pair of eyes to pair of eyes. She growls. A deep guttural noise from the back of her throat. "Yeah." She nods. "What's more Laissez-fuckin-faire than this?"

The crowd keeps its distance.

Athena smiles. "We're all dead. Doomed. But we just can't resist fuckin with each other, can we?" She frowns. Thinks of Michelle and her dumbass brother. Tightens her lips into a line. Forgets that. Marches to the bar.

The old man behind the counter doesn't ask anything.

Athena says, "Whiskey. Bottle."

The old man waits.

Athena pulls a short stack of cookies from her jacket. Lays it on the bar top.

The bartender's gaze snaps to the baked goods. He slides his fingers around em. Sniffs em. "Oh, Christ." He sniffs again. "Never thought I'd smell that again." Tears well in his eyes. "My mom...she..."

Athena snaps her fingers. Points to a bottle of Buffalo Trace. "I need that."

The bartender pulls himself away from the cookies' fragrance. "Yeah sure." He plants the full bottle in front of Athena.

She caresses the booze. Squints as the population of the bar surrounds her. Thinks: *Shit*. Thinks: *Having a doctor on this long haul wouldn't be a bad idea*. Says, "How well do you know the pimps and whores at the Motel 6?"

\* \* \*

Athena walks back to the Hellcat.

In the five minutes she spent inside, fifteen assholes have cluttered around her car and the pregnant idiot and the half-awake doctor she left on the asphalt near the Hellcat. Now there's shouting and some mad commotion.

Athena fires three times.

Big fat .45 slugs tear two spines and one head in half.

Athena spits.

The crowd freaks out. Voices shriek. They back away. None of em know each other well enough to form an offensive line against this psycho road runner.

Which's lucky.

Athena unlocks her door. Reaches in. Grabs the sawed-off shotgun. Trains it. Puts pellets in fleeing backs. "This's mine." She breaks the breach. Grips spent shells. Tosses em inside the Hellcat. Reloads. Flays more skin with clouds of scattered metal.

Michelle and Mark look to her with eyes ringed by tears.

Michelle's clothing is torn. Again.

Mark has fresh blood streaming from his lower lip.

Athena nods. "Room 219. Stay away from the pool unless you want every STD known to man."

# 6.

**"I** don't enjoy being my own patient."

These are the first words outta Mark's mouth. After Michelle helped him find his way upstairs and Athena kept watch. She scared the shit outta the pimps who wanted to talk loud or interfere.

Which is to say: She shot the bastards.

With that, both Mark and Athena understood who the other was. He, the stoic brother still operating in defense of his sister. She, a particular brand of crazy that's best left unchallenged.

Cuz when you're knee deep in blood and bone and ghosts and guns, well...

Welcome to the American Dream.

The rotten, cancerous nature of the beast.

Michelle cradles her brother's head in her lap. Both on the bed second from the door. The whole place is filthy and dilapidated and horrid. Cracks in the plaster. Stains on the walls and what remains of the carpet. All lit by the one functioning light in the ceiling that threatens to crumble at any given moment.

But it's a room. With two beds.

And a toilet that works.

Athena peels back the beige curtains of the room's window. Sucks her teeth. Stares out at the carnal carnage that goes on and on in the courtyard below. Along the walkways outside their room.

Frenzied humping and rubbing after the pimps and the johns work out their trades in the twilight hours. Bullets or brass for a blow job or a jerk off. Maybe something rare like candy or baby powder for a screw. Most going at it in the open. Some others prefer a curtain.

Time in the hotel itself is pricier.

Takes at least a stack of freshly baked cookies.

Or at least the *promise* of two dozen for the local business bosses. The piggish politicians—who Athena hasn't met yet and really doesn't want to—who control access to the bridge.

Hell, it's not like pols ever really *change* or act human.

Thing Athena's afraid of is becoming a commodity herself.

Some lump on one of these boss's payrolls who cranks out cookies for good boys.

Scares the shit outta her.

Mark coughs. His head bounces against the baby in Michelle's belly. He groans. Prods himself with professional fingers. Athena sees him wince as he tests putting pressure against two of his ribs.

He sighs. "Two cracked for sure. More bruised. I can't do anything about it, though. Next few weeks are gonna be painful and shitty."

"I'm not sure how that's any different than now," Michelle says.

Athena grunts. She returns her gaze to the Hellcat. It's parked almost directly below. Pulled back a bit from the building so she can watch it. It'll be fine. She even rigged a couple of spare batteries together so if anyone gets curious, they'll get electrocuted. Zap. Nothing but a fetid heap that draws flies. But she hates having it outta her sight all the same.

She duct tapes her sawed-off shotgun to the shabby dresser. Both barrels face the door. She threads a line of twine from both triggers to the doorknob. As with the car, anyone who opens it is in for a mean surprise.

Mark and Michelle watch. Both seemingly appreciative of Athena's...talents.

She grabs her drab green rucksack. A Coleman lantern. Heads into the bathroom without a word.

Mark and Michelle offer none of their own.

Athena shuts the flimsy plywood door behind her. Slides the bolt shut on the equally flimsy lock. She's in total darkness till she clicks on her lantern. Then she's bathed in fluorescent blue.

A pale ghost in a cracked mirror.

She pulls off her leather gloves. Unzips her black leather jacket. Slides it from her shoulders. Lays it on the tile near her pig-nosed boots. Athena pulls her dirty grey undershirt over her head. Plops it down on the jacket.

She's gotten used to her naked appearance in the mirror.

But it took years.

Years of watching the melanoma on her arm and under her left breast spread. So slow. So constant. Ever growing. Populating her body like the jagged scars that line her flesh.

This roadmap of pain.

Athena rubs an unscented disinfectant wipe between her breasts. She lifts and wipes underneath. Gets the grime and dead skin stink. Then goes over her armpits. She strips off her boots. Socks. Belt with spare magazines. Pistol and holster. Leather pants.

Men's boxer briefs—which she's always worn since they're far more comfortable than the women's equivalent and easier to come by.

She scrubs the rest of herself. And her face and head.

Then she sits on the toilet. Naked. To dry off and enjoy strained pissing and shitting somewhere other than the side of the road.

Athena grabs the Buffalo Trace from her rucksack. Pops the cork. Takes a swig. She licks her lips as it burns down her throat. A cigarette comes next. With long hot drags that mesh well with the heat of the whiskey.

When she's done, she drops the stogie in the toilet. It hisses in the water and excrement. Athena flushes. Gives herself another good disinfectant wipe between the thighs. Dresses. And heads into the room.

Where it doesn't look like Mark or Michelle have moved much at all.

Athena rests her rucksack next to her bed. Considers the contents for a moment. Sighs. Digs the toilet paper and the disinfectant wipes back out. Places em on Mark and Michelle's bed.

Mark struggles to sit up. But he does. Even if he's wincing and clutching his side.

A sad smile crosses Michelle's lips. She speaks in a slow, hesitant way. "Do...you have any food?" She rubs her belly.

Athena closes one eye at the pregnant woman. As though the other is peering through a sniper scope. She sniffs. Goes back into her pack. Produces a fat bag of dog jerky. She tosses it onto the other bed with a caveat: "That's mine."

Michelle nods. She takes a good palm of jerky. Enough to stave off hunger. But no more. Then Michelle reseals the bag and chews the muscle.

Mark does the same. He takes a proper proportion before he hands the dogmeat back to Athena. Who puts it back in its place in her ruck before sucking whiskey and lighting another cigarette.

Mark watches his sister wobble to the bathroom with a lantern.

Athena relaxes against her pillow—more than one and she feels smothered. She alternates between pulls of the American Spirit and the Buffalo Trace. She knows she'll need real water from the bottle in her bag soon, but the booze needs time to do its job too.

Mark finishes his dogmeat. Hisses as he readjusts himself on the bed and reclines against the pillows. "Before the germ hit, I was setting up my own practice in the Adirondacks. The mountains. Fifteen or twenty years ago, being some nice old country town doctor really seemed to fit the bill." He groans as he settles in. "I wanted some kind of quiet. Settle in. Live cheap and slowly pay back all those student loans that got me to be an MD." He smiles.

Looks to Athena.

Athena stares at the wall. Smokes. Drinks.

Mark clears his throat. "I had to live cheap, you know? I tried to save my money because I knew what kind of man my father was. Michelle's dad—my dad—the bastard would disappear every few years. Then I'd learn I had a new brother or sister. I tried to meet them all, see if I could help them. But the only one I ever really connected with was Michelle. God, and she's half my age." Mark scratches his head. Considers it. "Michelle's mom died before...everything ended. I can't remember exactly when—it's hard to remember. And then she came to live with me. I thought I could keep her safe, you know? Or I thought, at least, that life with me was better than assuming our dad would do the decent thing. I admit that I kept her too isolated. Too 'safe' from the realities of this world now..." Mark looks to Athena again. "What did you... What were you doing before?"

Athena breathes smoke. Sees David in her head. Flicks ash on the floor. "Mechanic."

Mark nods. "Was that the family trade? You don't see many female mechanics."

Athena takes a pull of whiskey. Eyes still locked on the wall. She says, "Does everyone in your goddamn genetic line have a problem with word vomit? Does silence scare the shit outta you or something?"

Mark frowns. "No... I..." He sinks into the bed. Lies back. Stops looking at Athena. Watches the ceiling. "No."

He doesn't say anything else.

They sit in relative silence.

The sounds of violent glee outside are interrupted only by Michelle's flush of the toilet. Her footsteps as she returns to the bed and chances a peek under the covers then braves the comfort of a blanket.

Mark frowns.

Athena sees his eyes flit to her for a brief moment before he shuts em. His chest rises with labored effort. Lungs clutching as much air as they can before they push against damaged ribs and send hot shots of pain through him.

She knows how it feels. Thinks about it. Bites her cigarette. Leans over the bed. Reaches into her bag. Produces aspirin in a wax paper pouch. Two of em. She plants both small packages on the half-broken fiberboard end table between the beds. Slams the bottle of whiskey down.

Mark's eyes snap open. He props himself up on his elbows.

Grabs the two pouches of painkillers. Studies em before popping the pills. He washes it down with whiskey.

Booze being the safest thing to drink nowadays. Can't always trust the water.

He squints at the taste. Sniffs. Wipes at the liquid that flushes his eyes.

Then he takes another healthy chug. Coughs. And corks the bottle.

Athena stands. Turns off the lights. Smokes.

And stares out the window at her car.

When she's drunk enough, she looks at the shape of Michelle's belly.

And feels something like envy.

# 7.

The morning is shattered by shots. The staccato of machine gun fire. Big engines that come pouring into Love's Travel Stop at the break of dawn.

Athena rolls off her bed. Hits the floor as rounds hammer the motel. The window explodes. She's showered with glass.

She sneers. Throws herself forward. Unloops the twine from the shotgun's triggers. Rips the sawed-off from its duct tape mooring on the dresser.

Mark and Michelle scurry for cover. He pushes her down and covers her body. She doesn't scream the way she did before, but there's a stark look of terror on her face.

Athena snaps her fingers. Gets Mark's attention. Snaps her fingers again and again and points to her rucksack.

He nods. Loops one of the straps around his palm.

Michelle clutches Mark's plaid shirt.

Mark hisses through his teeth as he rises to a crouch. Hisses more as he hefts the bag and helps his sister into the same stance.

They wait. Watch.

Athena pauses. Takes a deep breath. Two. Motions for Mark and Michelle to stay put. Stands and approaches the door. She listens as booted feet stomp through the courtyard below. Then as more mount the stairs and launch attacks on all the rooms they come across.

Screams. Shouts.

Bursts of gunfire.

Crashing glass.

The thuds of bodies hitting the ground.

Some crazy full-throated motherfucker outside on a bullhorn telling people they "...don't understand who they're fighting."

But in addition to all that, Athena hears combat. Road runners waging war against...whoever.

Love's ruthless population ain't thrilled about the early morning incursion.

Boots stop in front of Athena's door. There's a lull in the air and she can imagine a raider on the other side rearing back to kick the door in.

Which they do.

Wood splinters on its hinges.

The lock flies free.

The raider's there. His right leg still in the air from the kick.

Athena pulls both triggers.

The blast sends the raider tumbling backward with a flash of gore. Torn flesh and broken ribs. Guts spraying like party favors. He goes over the railing. Just shy of the Hellcat. Lands on his neck. His bleeding body comes to a rest with the head at entirely the wrong angle.

Athena breaks open the shotgun. Yanks the spent shells and

drops em. Reloads. Switches the sawed-off to her left hand. Her right holds the 1911 Mil-Spec.

She rolls out into the morning air. Ducks against the short wall of a railing along the catwalk. Tries to assess what the hell is going on—since, so far, she's only really gotten to: Shoot everyone. Get to the car.

And that's her basic line of thinking anyway.

Athena peers through a gap in the wall.

Pimps and whores play defense. They shoot over and *through* johns. Guys who were getting their rocks off suddenly find themselves full of unhealthy holes.

One of the raiders is a true-blue loon. He runs rampant from victim to victim. Machete high in the air. Before it comes down into a pimp's neck. Unleashes a torrent of red.

The bullhorn bastard croons. "The men of the Iron Cross—"

Athena groans. "Fuck me."

"—seek only retribution."

She'd chalk this up to stupid happenstance except the raiders were set up on I-80. So she was gonna run into the pricks one way or the other. Doesn't matter that Michelle and Mark were there.

Though it does complicate things.

Athena huffs.

Does it?

Easy enough to leap over the edge. Catch the railing.

Bail.

Leave these two fools with her rucksack and get going with the real prize: The Hellcat.

Athena shakes her head. She may be a bitch. But not a *fuckin* bitch.

Just enough of a bitch to get this thing done right.

And she can't really bear the idea of letting something useful like a doctor in the wastes go to waste.

She blinks.

*Get it done right.*

With these two.

Lousy proposition.

Athena bites her lip and waves Mark and Michelle forward.

They get to the doorframe. Halt.

Athena fires twice with the 1911. Puts .45 bullets through the throat and cheek of some Iron Cross asshole running at her from the left. Fires twice more with the shotgun and flays the flesh of two Iron Cross assholes loping along from the right.

She reloads the shotgun. Eyeballs Mark and Michelle. "I don't know what life made you. But I know what it made me." She motions em forward. Hands the pregnant woman the sawed-off stuffs another four twelve-gauge shells into the brunette's front hoodie pockets. Says, "Kicks hard. Mark can't use it. His ribs are fucked enough as it is. But you could be blind as hell and still hit someone." She grabs her rucksack from Mark.

The black bastard on the bullhorn squawks: "We're only here for the interloper. She took something of ours. She killed our kind."

This motherfucker. He stands on the flatbed of an idling Ford pickup between the Motel 6 and Love's proper. Back of the bed is weighed down—maybe by design, for traction—by a six-foot Iron Cross. Skulls with that forehead ink adorn the grill of the truck and the cross.

Athena grunts. Jumps the railing. Catches the concrete catwalk floor with her gloved fingers. Drops to the asphalt below.

Iron Cross goons swarm.

They shriek. "The car. *Get the car.*"

Athena cocks an eye as four move in to surround her.

A fifth chuckles. Saunters. Stupid goddamn forehead an advertisement for the Iron Cross. He grips the handle on the driver's side door.

And squeals.

Amps provide the power. Volts dance through his body. Char his heart. He drops. A Kentucky Fried Fuck.

The Iron Cross goons turn to watch the smoldering remains of their ruined compatriot.

Athena snap-shoots em from the hip. Whether they're looking or not. Nice quick bullets from her Springfield piece that pierce their brains as Mark and Michelle rush down the stairs nearby.

Athena screams. More guttural than anything else. "Now. We go *now*." She slams her palms against the top of the Hellcat.

The shotgun in Michelle's hands goes off once.

Twice.

She shrieks as the gun bucks and a goon topples.

Athena looks over the carnage. All this crazy shit cuz of a car and some Semtex.

Cuz of her, really.

These Iron Cross bastards have serious *numbers*. And hardware. Enough of both to take on a pretty well stocked and armed place like Love's.

The bastard with the bullhorn points to Athena. Out there at the outskirts. He points to Athena and the Hellcat and Mark and Michelle.

Athena uses a gloved hand to open her door and shut off the electrocution batteries. They're probably drained from nuking the screwhead goon anyway, but frying Mark and Michelle wouldn't sit right with Athena.

She's gotta protect her investments.

The two siblings fight to get into the goddamn backseat of the car so they can be gone.

And the bastard with the bullhorn shouts to his followers: "Dodge. Black. The bitch is in the Dodge. *Seize her and her machine.*"

Athena licks her lips. Slides into the driver's seat. She turns the big engine over. Looks over the seat at Michelle and the shotgun. "Ammo at your feet." She reverses across the asphalt. "Knock out the back windows if you need to."

She throws the Hellcat into gear. Rubber screams against the ground.

All Athena thinks is, *Fuck you fuck you fuck you fuck fuck.*

The Hellcat peels out from its parking spot. A roaring animal.

An animal all the Iron Cross cocksuckers want a piece of.

Demented Fords and the batshit bullhorn bastard and Chevys and Hondas and Mazdas pour onto the road in Athena's rear view mirror.

And so, fuck you, Athena pours on the Hellcat's horsepower then cuts it on the corners. Works the brakes and the gas. So that the fucknut with the bullhorn and his driver in the Ford pickup have a hard time keeping up.

She curves right. Brings the whole party back to I-80.

Some goon from the sidelines hurls a brick at the Hellcat. It shatters the passenger side window. The bars keep it from landing inside. But Mark and Michelle cover their faces against the onslaught of safety glass.

Athena tosses her 1911 and two mags into the backseat.

Shouts, "Reload those. I need em reloaded."

Michelle's still coming to grips with the sawed-off. The terrifying power. The fact that she *killed someone* at the motel.

Li'l pregnant her.

She's mystified.

Mark looks around the backseat. "Where's the ammo?" He digs into one of the seatbacks. Finds a cotton pouch with loose ammo. Checks em and starts to slide .45 cartridges into the magazines.

At least he has some familiarity with firearms.

Some usefulness.

The Hellcat's tires choke on loose gravel for a heartbeat when they hit the bridge across the Susquehanna.

The men who used to be in charge and holding the line scurry for cover. Their rifles go down as the Hellcat passes. Then come up again against the members of the Iron Cross give chase.

Gunshots ring out.

Athena sees goons drop in the rearview mirror. Windshield glass shatters. A Honda veers off at the loss of its driver. Smashes against the side of a Chevy SUV. Which goes even further askew and slams into a concrete barrier. It's like playing pinball with heavy trucks.

So that's two vehicles down outta twenty.

The rest are all on the Hellcat's ass.

Athena growls. Pushes the gas.

The Hellcat hits sixty in under four seconds. Then seventy. Ninety. One-ten.

The Susquehanna River below is a blur of brown. They ride like a full-metal nightmare over the bridge. Some kinda industry on the right and the ticky tacky developments on the left are smudges of grey and white.

A Kawasaki crotch-rocket veers up on Athena's left. The lanky fuck riding whips a chain around.

She shouts to Mark, "*Gimme the gun.*" She reaches over the seat with her right hand. He left is locked around the steering wheel, keeping the Dodge on track.

He pops the seventh round into the first magazine. Loads the 1911. Racks the slide in a rush. He hands her the pistol.

Athena takes her gun. Uses the butt to bash her window out. Doesn't need it anyway.

The motorcycle goon gets close on his nitro-boosted suicide machine. He whips a chain around his hands. Pulls his arm back to obliterate her windshield.

Athena fires three times out the window. One .45 round hits his gas tank. Another goes wild. The last one hammers into a face hidden behind a hockey mask with the Iron Cross on it.

As for accuracy: Fuck you. Try driving and shooting.

The cyclist drops from his bike. Tumbles and skids to a bloody stop on asphalt that's like sandpaper on flesh. His two-wheeled machine shoots off into the woods. Smashes against a tree.

The other goons ain't dissuaded in the least.

Athena shouts. "There're more empty mags in my seatback. Load em."

This while they scream along I-80.

The green of trees give way to the mud brown of untended farmlands.

A motherfucker Athena doesn't see on her right leaps from his bike. Onto the hood. He slams his face into the windshield. Once. Twice. A seam splits in his forehead. Doesn't bother him. He keeps pounding the glass with his skull.

Athena sneers. Jukes the car. Hopes to slide him off with inertia. Little to the right. Little to the left.

But the fucker's on like a bug. Won't budge.

He grips the lip of the hood near the windshield. Locks his fingers to the knuckle. Rears back. Swings a pipe.

Athena puts her gun to the glass. Fires four times.

Two splatter his guts. The third shot goes nowhere. The fourth burrows through his teeth and out the back of his head.

The goon's face is briefly frozen in a flash. This weird dumb shock of an incoming sneeze.

Then inertia takes him and his body tumbles away.

First under the Hellcat's rear wheels.

Then under the Mazdas and Fords chasing.

The spider web cracks make it hard as hell to see out the front.

Athena throws the gun back into the backseat. "More bullets." She reaches into her door's well. Grabs another satchel of loose ammo. Tosses it to Mark.

Mark drops the mag from her 1911 into his lap. All spent except one bullet in the chamber. He locks more .45 rounds into place. Does it feverishly.

A blue Chevy Camaro slams into the Hellcat. Tries to bash it from the right. Push the big Dodge beast off the road. Two lunatic goons in the front seat. The passenger climbs out his window and scuttles across the Chevy's hood. A manic spider.

Athena hits the brakes in time to see the spider-man miss her car and get chewed up by the wheels.

*Thump thump.*

She hits the gas again and they jump from sixty to ninety.

Athena's brain howls.

*Okay. Okay. Let's go. Let's push this as far is it can go.*

There's a growl in her throat.

The speedometer hits one-twenty.

The bullhorn bastard in her rearview fades.

A dirty white Accord pounds her left side.

Michelle sticks the shotgun out. Pulls the first trigger. Then the second. And the inside of the Accord is painted red.

It stutters and drifts. Front end hits a ditch. Stops so brutally that anybody inside is gonna be missing vertebrae.

Athena chances a look back at her pregnant cargo. Offers the brunette a thumbs-up.

The road turns ahead. Athena takes her foot off the gas. Coasts.

Not just to save some fuel but to give the Iron Cross idiots a chance to catch up so she can see what they might plan. Maybe kill enough more that they'll piss off.

She doesn't have any particular desire to merely *flee*.

She wants em dead.

Otherwise, pricks like this'll just hound em.

And fuck that noise.

She has no intention of driving to California with bastards on her tail.

Athena watches the rearview. Licks her lips. Adjusts her ass in the seat and checks her grip on the steering wheel. She mumbles a wish to the goon with the bullhorn, "Follow me Tonto."

Goons' cars round the bend. They appear like phantoms on the grey road behind her.

She moves the car between wrecks. Hits the gas again. Farmland blows by. Then more greenery. Trees and bushes that encroach on the blacktop.

Deer gallop into the line of fire.

Athena doesn't let off the gas, but she curses the damn things. "Fuck off fuck off *fuck off*." And her passenger side mirror barely misses one's fluffy rear.

Next deer ain't so lucky.

The Hellcat's bull-bar plows into the doe's side. At the back right thigh. It cripples the shitty animal immediately. Sends the body bouncing off the hood. Into the windshield. Cracks the glass more. The fuzzy fuck sails over the car. Flops to the blacktop behind em.

A pursuing motorcycle hits the carcass. The front wheel slams to a stop. The rider flies. End over end. He lands on his head. The ground shoves his chin into his chest and his skin tears away.

Athena sniffs. Drives with one hand. Reaches the other into the backseat.

Mark hands her the reloaded 1911. He gets to work stuffing rounds into the other spare magazines. So there're three more in reserve.

A Ford pickup truck rushes to the tail of the Hellcat. It's driver screams with glee. Pounds the front dash. Like he's coaxing the vehicle to surge faster. A goon in the flatbed jumps and crows and slaps the roof of the cab in a manic drum beat.

He hefts and aims a spear gun at the Dodge's tires.

Athena jukes. Tries to keep the spear gunner from getting a good target.

The Hellcat's tires squeal in protest.

When they tear onto a straight stretch of highway, Athena opens her door and leans out. Right hand keeps the wheel steady. Left hand aims the heavy metal of her 1911.

She opens up on the spear gun goon.

He takes two slugs to the chest. Blood sprays from him and the whipping wind turns it into a fine mist that flutters away.

Athena pours .45-caliber rounds against the Ford's front window. It cracks. Splinters. Starts to fall apart. And the last shot finally punches where it's supposed to and sends the driver's nose through the back of his head with a splash of red.

She hands Mark the pistol.

He drops the empty mag on the seat. Reloads. Makes sure there's a bullet in the chamber before returning it.

Michelle unloads a double dose of buckshot into the driver of a speedy Mazda that threatens to ram em. Her wrists jerk with the force of the blast, but she doesn't shriek.

Gunfire from the goons rattles the back of the Hellcat. A few rounds pepper the rear window.

Mark throws himself over his sister to protect her.

Athena stomps down on the gas again.

They play this game. Mile after mile. Along I-80.

And Athena starts to wonder when the raiders are gonna run outta gas.

Hell, she wonders when *she's* gonna run outta gas.

All the acrobatics she's asked the car to do has hit her fuel reserves pretty hard. She's burned too much gas dealing with these goons. Little less than half left now.

Seventy miles of shooting and juking.

It'll be a problem soon.

But after another barrage from the 1911. Another hail that ruins cars and glass and faces. The goons back off. Either low on fuel or in need of wound-licking.

Athena keeps the Hellcat going one-ten.

She ain't optimistic enough to assume the goons are done, though. They won't leave her alone at this point. Everyone's too invested in seeing her demise—Athena included—but this's a welcome reprieve.

If she can hack it for the next hundred she'll be happy. That'll put her close to empty, sure. Also puts her at the western border of Pennsylvania, though. There should be somewhere near the edge she can refuel. And a hundred miles of distance between the Hellcat and the goons is nothing to sneeze at.

It'll take the cocksuckers a while to catch up. Stands to reason as well that they'll keep on I-80. So she'll have to find a reasonable detour. Get the Hellcat in a good spot where it can't be ambushed. Just in case.

Always possible that the goons are more clever than they look. So she rides the Hellcat hard. And fast.

And they end up somewhere north of a place called Turkey City. That's what it says on the map, for fuck's sake. Turkey City. Where there's a dozen houses and the remains of a Post Office that the local wildlife have taken as their own.

Michelle blinks at the vacant view. The bones and scraps of cloth that haven't yet been plucked up by scavengers. Raccoons that rear up on their hind legs. Rodents the size of dogs. They play their fingers together and wonder—with black-eyed, very human expressions—just what the fuck these noisy interlopers want.

Athena follows the back roads south. Got another thirty or forty miles in the tank. But they need fuel soon. Damn soon.

Michelle says, "There's nothing here."

Mark licks his lips. Stares out the window.

Michelle repeats: "There's nothing here at all."

Athena sneers. She doesn't wanna get back on I-80. She looks for red tanks in backyards and repair shops. Some signifying agent that gasoline is nearby.

She finds it on a rural road overrun by grass. Turns the Hellcat onto some fucker's lawn. Farther back. Asphalt goes from blacktop to green to dusty dirt and gravel.

The big matte-black beast rumbles to a stop between a house and a barn and a single standing gas pump.

The air around em is quiet. Still.

Athena steps out. Dust clouds her boots. She walks to the solo pump. Smells it. The hose. Nozzle. Then cranks the primer at the side of the standup station.

Athena listens to the pump. She hears liquid under pressure in the hose.

Mark steps outta the Hellcat. Stretches like his life depends on it. A hand at his side. Where those ribs are messed up. He says, "Gasoline degrades."

Athena nods. Drags the nozzle over to the Hellcat's tank. "Yeah." She nods again. "The additives. The shit that's supposed to make it last longer." She looks at the Dodge lovingly. "I'll have to clean the fuel filter. Fuel lines. Maybe flush the engine." She sticks an American Spirit between her lips. Lights it. Grins. Pounds the hood of the Hellcat. "But if it burns, it burns."

Mark crosses his arms. Winces. "I understand where you're trying—"

"No." Athena shakes her head. "Don't."

Now Mark nods. "If that fuel is no good—"

"Then I kill myself and you can wait and watch the raiders catch up with us." She shrugs. "Not how I wanna go out, but it's better than the alternatives. I'd suggest shooting your sister next. Then yourself. Otherwise, maybe *they* shoot you low and *make you watch* while they rape your sister and tear her baby from her belly then rape it too." Athena smiles. "You, Herr Doktor, can stand there and ruminate on how this species you dedicated so much time to understand on a physical level is fucked psychologically." Athena spits. Puffs her cigarette.

Mark rolls his tongue around in his cheek. "You're sure about that?"

The fuel line chokes. Coughs. Athena taps it against the lip of the Hellcat's tank. Takes a full drag from her cigarette then flicks the Spirit away. She cocks an eye at Mark. Says, "Heroes don't last long out here, bud. No matter what you're thinking." Gas rushes into the car.

Mark groans. "But we *need* heroes. That's part of who we are."

Athena squints. "Heroes die."

"We're *all* going to die. That's the position of the planet now. Why not do...*something* to help the species."

Athena snorts. Chuckles. "You're here out of a basic need. That's all. You might be useful to me. Your sister might be useful to me." She walks the gas nozzle back to the pump. "Don't ever think otherwise."

* * *

Athena looks over the supplies in the trunk. Other than the copious amount of .45 ammo she put in the goons, they're fine. Enough, probably, to carry em through the Midwest wasteland without opening the doors except to steal gas.

She slams the trunk. Sighs at all the cosmetic damage the Hellcat took. Sees Michelle through the spider webs of the rear window.

The pregnant woman plays with the crank radio. Winds it up. Sticks her ear to the speaker.

Athena struts to the driver side door. Opens it and sits behind the wheel sideways so her feet rest on the dusty ground. Heels down. Boot tips up.

She lights a cigarette.

Michelle says, "Are you sure this thing works?"

Athena nods. "Yeah." She takes a drag. "But I haven't used the damn thing in weeks." She blows smoke. "There's never anything good on the radio anyway." She lifts her USB hard drive. "I don't unplug this anymore."

"Okay, but, like—" Michelle shakes the radio. Keeps cranking it "—there might be stuff we need to know." She plays with the dial.

Athena leans back. Stretches her spine. Her slender ribs uncomfortable between the arm rest on her left and the shifter to her left. Her head hits the ass area of the padded passenger seat.

She reaches behind her. Opens the passenger side door. Ashes her cigarette out there. Over her head. Then places the cancer stick back between her lips.

Michelle yells, "I got something." A big bright voice like a child's. As though she's accomplished something. Which Athena doesn't think she has.

So Athena grunts and sits back up and listens to the voice on the radio.

Probably the same dipshit crap that's always broadcast. Automated hits.

Athena smokes. Stares at the ground.

When the world died, radio died even harder. In 2015, it was already being run more by machines than humans. Auto-selecting "popular hits" that were assumed should be sent out into the ether. Maybe there was some voice to assure you that, yeah, sure, DJs *exist*. But it was always some corporatized computer that decided what to play next.

Like Phil Dick's *Radio Free Albemuth* writ huge.

The nightmare of machines and businesses telling you what to listen to.

And you had no choice.

That's why Athena gave up on radio *in toto*.

Better to have some classics playing from a solid state drive than be subjected to Taylor Swift. Maroon 5. Rihanna. Skrillex with his smattering of musical abortions. Selena *fuckin* Gomez or that rotten bitch Iggy Azalea.

Athena rubs her eyes in exhaustion at the thought that Justin Bieber might've survived the germ and is still running around, ruining the ears of anyone nearby.

The heart of the matter remains: Radio went to Shit Town and never came back.

Now Michelle is resurrecting the thing in the Hellcat's backseat.

Athena listens as the radio squawks:

"—so here at the edge of the wastes, well, it's a shitshow. Beaver Valley went bad and so did Perry. And Davis-Besse. And Enrico Fermi. Do I need to go on? Ohio's in pretty rough shape, my friends. As always, avoid Doc Frankie if you can. Do *not* go anywhere near Perry. We've gotten word that he has some freaky new contraption to *clean* the highways. And the Iron Cross boys are up in arms. Of course, we thought we were pretty lucky in Columbus until all the muties from the Great Lakes started swarming. Bugs. Fun fun. So your weather on the tens is...not great." Laughter. "Same as usual. Good luck out there, road runners. Here's Jefferson Airplane with 'Somebody To Love.' I'm Dapper Dan."

Athena arches her eyebrows. Looks into the backseat at Michelle. "Useful, huh?"

Michelle grimaces. "How was none of that useful to you? There is still a world out there."

Athena blows smoke. "Doesn't change a goddamn thing."

"So you're just gonna... Just gonna roll ahead. The radio people *know* things. The...the reporters." Michelle blinks. Stares at the backseat. "Journalists." She furrows her brow. "That's what they were, right?"

"I remember journalism." Athena pulls herself from the front seat. Stretches. "Doesn't have anything to do with us, though."

"They say we're headed right for the wasteland. And Doctor Frankie."

"Along I-80, yeah. Thousand-mile stretch through the radiated zones. It's the shortest route. *My* plan remains the same, in spite of you and your brother."

Michelle rubs her stomach. Shakes her head. "Is...that going to hurt us?"

Athena takes a drag. Talks with smoke flowing between her teeth. "Yeah. It's gonna hurt."

# 8.

The sun approaches the horizon.

They eat dog jerky and drink water.

Athena doesn't wanna get back on the highway till enough time has passed for the goons to either give up or totally overshoot em. She thinks that *they* think she'll have kept on. Wouldn't expect her to burn a whole day of travel waiting around.

But she absolutely will.

Gives her a chance to bake and prep Semtex bricks and key the detonator and check the car and lament the amount of damage it's sustained. None of which she'll be able to fix without a garage.

At least the bars in the windows are still there.

Michelle stays glued to the crank radio. She never does find anything other than that Dapper guy. But that's fine, since the station seems dedicated to playing decent music.

Athena doesn't care so long as the pregnant woman keeps her mouth shut.

For his part, Mark rummages through two nearby houses and returns with blankets for himself and his sister. He offers one to her in the back seat. Says, "There are raccoons and cats around here the size of prized hogs." He sports a bemused look.

Michelle nods half-heartedly. Takes the blanket. Keeps searching the dial.

Athena puts her hands on her hips. "Did you bring back meat?"

Mark shakes his head. "No... What?"

"You said there are cats and coons the size of hogs. Why didn't you bring back meat?"

"I..." Mark shrugs. "I just didn't think—"

Athena scoffs. She stomps to the trunk. Grabs a razor-sharp Buck knife. Loops it and its holster onto her belt. Then she plucks a few more 1911 mags from Mark's refills in the back seat.

Michelle's still there. Fucking with the radio. Barely paying attention.

And Mark stands looking useless in the dirt.

Athena heads for the nearest house. A two-story white thing. Not special in any way. Only decrepit like everything else.

She slows her pace and pushes in the side door. Pistol up in her right hand. Flashlight in her left.

Long-forgotten pictures of a family that once-was decorate the dingy dining room she passes through. Plates with food long gone. Silverware scattered haphazardly. Even the remains of bones.

The idea that these people were enjoying dinner when the germs scurried across the country barely touches her mind. It enters her brain and flees.

Athena creeps along. Quiet as she can be. Following the beam of light.

She listens for animals. The scraping of their nails against deteriorating wood and cheap linoleum.

There's some farther along. Around the corner. In the body of this dead house.

So Athena keeps her creep. Steps light. Rounds the corner to the left.

Mark wasn't lying, at least.

There's a small family of raccoons poking their head out from the remains of a couch. Their torn-apart nest. Their eyes are bright reflective discs in the flashlight's glare.

She counts six. Three little ones and three big ones. Some kinda breeding trio.

They don't run at the sight of her. They stare. Unsure.

Till Athena puts a .45 round through one of the big ones' skulls.

It drops and the others scamper for safer parts of the house.

She kicks it with a stubby boot to make sure it's dead. Then grabs it by a hind leg. Drags it back to the side door. Outside. She hefts the fifty-pound monstrosity and plants it on her right shoulder. Doesn't want the damn thing to get filthy with dirt and dust and stone.

Athena grunts and drops it on the trunk hood of the Hellcat.

Michelle looks back with a wide-eyed face through the windowless rear of the car.

Athena takes a deep breath. Lights a cigarette. Nods to Mark. "Fire."

Mark nods back. He hobbles off toward the trees for stones and dry branches and tinder.

Athena moves the coon carcass so it's flat on its back atop the trunk. Its face slacks back against the rear bars.

And Michelle can't help but stare at its dead eyes as Athena gets to work.

The road runner grabs the animal's dick and balls among its fur. Flicks open her Buck knife. Slices off the cock and its two spermy compatriots. She flips the critter and makes a shallow insertion from its ass to its throat along the spine. She digs the knife in. Careful to make sure she can strip its hide but not puncture any organs.

All the while, blood spills and pools.

And Michelle stares horrified. Now clutching the radio as if good music will save her from reality.

She flips the coon back over. Splits its sternum. Opens the chest cavity. She reaches inside and grabs the esophagus. Cuts it close to the base of the skull. Then works backward. She removes the internal organs with quick flicks of the Buck blade. All the tissue that keeps it stuck inside the raccoon.

Anything inedible is tossed. She doesn't bother with the organs.

Athena finds the urethra and the bladder. Makes sure to pinch and slice the piss-filled thing so it doesn't contaminate the meat. She carries that whole mess away from the coon carcass. Chucks it into the weeds—which she'll burn after dinner. Walks back. Finishes the job. Tilts the dead thing. Lets its blood drain out and *pitter-patter* against the dirt like awful rain.

The hide she can use. So she cuts along the inside of the legs. Right down to the paws. Peels back the skin. Always slicing at the membrane that sticks the hide to the muscle.

Athena places all the hide to the side. Near Michelle's freaked out face.

Now she's left with fatty, red remains that just need to be freed of their glands.

Mark returns. Glances at his sister. The uncaring Athena.

He builds a fire pit a safe distance from the Hellcat.

Athena sniffs. Wipes her nose with her sleeve. She turns to the fire pit and ignites the kindling with one of her many black and white Bic disposable lighters.

When the fire rages properly, she hoists a long grill grate from the trunk. Lays it across burning wood. Then slaps the coon carcass on top of that.

It sizzles.

Michelle peels herself from the backseat of the car. "I need water."

Athena cocks an eye at her. "You need blood and meat." She gestures to the roasting raccoon. "Fresh flesh to nourish the parasite in your belly."

Michelle teeters a tad. Almost leans against the Hellcat. Catches herself. A weak smile attempts to cross her lips.

The crank radio screams. Shocks the pregnant woman from her respite.

Mark scowls. A sad look with a furrowed brow. "What the hell is that?"

Insane warbling. And laughter. All of it echoed and distorted over the little black plaster radio in the car. The dry heaves of a body that wants to puke. The muttering and snorting of a large animal. Then wet chewing. Chewing. Chewing. Grunts. More chewing. Liquid splashes. Drips. Then deep guttural groans and sighs of pleasure.

Satisfaction.

Michelle reaches a palsied hand inside the Hellcat.

Shuts the radio off.

Athena stares at her car. The corners of her lips vacillate between sneer and frown. She looks to the dirt. Then makes sure all the mags for her 1911 are full.

# 9.

The Hellcat purrs.

Athena turns it back onto I-80. West.

And everything seems fine till Michelle reminds Athena that they're heading for the radiated zones.

That's when the goons reappear. They pour in behind the Hellcat about ten miles outside Turkey fuckin City.

And everything gets real weird.

"They saw the fire," Mark says. "Saw the fire or heard your pistol go off inside the house. Then they just waited for us."

Athena grunts. Stomps the gas pedal. Readjusts her safety goggles.

Like the "how" of any this shit matters now.

She hears the dark-skinned man she calls Bullhorn behind her. "We won't kill the man or the cow. But the Iron Cross demands penitence."

Athena grins at the rearview mirror. Nods in agreement.

Penitence. Sure.

She tosses a brick of Semtex out her window. It slaps against the asphalt behind the Hellcat. She waits for an incoming Honda to get its grill in front of it. Hits the detonator.

Watches as a fat gut-rocking explosion lifts the Honda up from the front and flips it onto its roof like a pathetic turtle.

Other goon vehicles dash and dodge around the wreckage.

Something flutters and bounces off the hood of the Hellcat. A green abomination the size of a small dog. An insect. Grasshopper or locust. It gets caught in the forward bars of the rollcage. Mandibles mashing together. *Click click*. It chitters and squeaks.

Athena pulls her 1911. Fires.

The bug's head explodes in a spray of chitin and juice.

She spits the yellow ichor that gets in her mouth out the side window.

The insect body flaps away with the wind. Tumbles on the road.

Bullhorn hollers. "Bugs! Bugs! We're approaching the radiated zone."

Athena grabs another Semtex brick. Chucks it. Switches the detonator to "2." Pulls the trigger. Enjoys another glorious explosion of flame and wrecked metal and ruined enemy bodies. Flesh shredded in bloody booms and cracked blacktop.

Mark reaches over the seat. Grabs the rest of the Semtex. Plucks the detonator from Athena's hand. "Just drive."

Athena can't argue with it.

She lowers her head and watches the white-lined nightmare ahead.

Push it. Harder. Faster. Farther.

The Hellcat coughs on bad fuel.

Athena shouts. Yells. She bangs her hands against the steering wheel. Then clamps back on tight. Even with the RPM loss, she can still outrun the goons. Just gotta crank it on.

Which's Right and True and Good.

Except there's something in front of her.

She blinks. Squints.

It's a wall that isn't a wall. A machine built to resemble the upper half of a chrome skeleton that stares with two big red eyes and arms that span the whole width of I-80 near Mercer. The mad thing waits around a south-turning bend in the road. Hunched between the north and south tree lines. Shiny arms angled in a push-up position.

The skull is full of teeth. Jaw half-open. The chrome inside lit by blue lights. Flat gleaming metal where the nose might be. The bottom of its rib cage rests on the pavement. Supported by a series of wheels the size of tractor tires.

The bone machine locks the endless, unblinking red pools of its eyes on the Hellcat. It roars. Screams. The sound itself akin to a badly encoded digital bass note.

For the first time in her life, Athena slams on the brakes out of panic.

Goons shoot by her in a cloud of burnt rubber that stinks to high hell.

Then their tail lights all blink on in that same kinda panic.

Michelle whimpers. Digs her nails into the seat in front of her.

The big bone machine snaps up the smaller vehicles of the goons and stuffs em into a strange metal basket built onto its back. Fine black tendrils like electrical cords pluck the occupants out and shove em into its mouth.

Their bodies—alive and shrieking—bounce down a pipe into

the ribcage and land in a different container. When they hit the bottom, they're restrained by more whipping cables.

Athena spins the wheel. Floors it. Peels out. Turns the Hellcat east.

Whatever fresh hell this is, she doesn't want any part of it.

The speedometer ramps up. But the car coughs again on bad fuel and her RPMs drop further.

Athena screams anew.

Mark hurls Semtex behind them but it detonates too soon. All he manages to destroy is asphalt.

The bone machine crawls on. It manages to cover more ground than Athena can.

If she hadn't been *chased* into the damn thing...

If she hadn't insisted on filling the car with shitty gas...

The bone machine lunges. Locks gleaming metal fingers around the Hellcat. The car stops dead. Engine and tires growl and shriek in a vain attempt to escape the machine's grasp.

Tendrils slither around the doors. Seek out the handles and open em. Then they wrap themselves around Mark. Michelle.

Athena hacks at one with her Buck knife to no avail. She ends up struggling and shouting in the air like everyone else. Then in the bone machine's sleek mouth. Where a new set of tendrils disarm her. Then toss her down a metal gullet lit by blue LEDs.

She presses her hands against the sides to slow her descent. Day can't get much worse, but a broken collar bone or leg or arm sure as shit won't help things.

The enormous robot regards the Hellcat. Holds it up as though it's a cherished relic. It tucks the car gently into the compartment on its back.

Instead of chucking Michelle into the rib pit, the bone machine lowers her. Slow. Careful.

Athena squints at this. Decides she doesn't trust or like that very much at all.

She casts her eyes around at the others taken prisoner. Mark. Michelle. Thirty goons sporting forehead tattoos in various stages of either adrenaline or drug fury. Their eyes wide and crazy and locked on her.

Then there's Bullhorn. The big mouthy bastard.

He smiles.

Athena rushes toward him to kick his teeth in.

Cables snap her up before she can.

The goons chuckle.

Bullhorn keeps his goddamn grin on.

Blue lights in the rib cage flash to red.

Gas flushes into the air.

And everyone gets real tired, real fast.

# 10.

Athena groans. Her vision swims as her body fights to shake off whatever sleep agent was forced on her. She rubs her eyes. Feels around go get a sense of where she is.

There's an old mattress under her ass. One next to two others. Metal flooring nearby. And metal walls...and a metal ceiling with one far-too-bright bulb that makes her blink and wince.

She sees the door. Bars outside the reinforced window.

Like a prison.

Is she in prison?

What the fuck is going on.

Athena shakes her head. Knocks her skull around a bit with her fists. Uses some of the pain to refocus.

She sniffs. Stands. Listens.

Tony goddamn Bennett is crooning over the speaker in the upper corner of the room. His version of Hank Williams' "Cold, Cold Heart."

Athena mumbles, "You gotta be fuckin kidding."

At least she still has her clothes.

She walks to the door. Presses her face against the glass. Lays her ear against it. Hopes to hear something other than Bennett's voice.

Can't.

She jumps back when a shape passes by.

A man, she thinks. A guard. Human but...off.

Athena digs into her pockets. Pants and jacket. Hopes they left her with something.

Nope.

Of course not.

Why would she be that fuckin lucky?

Athena balls her fists. Clamps her mouth shut. Forces herself to breathe through her nose so she doesn't hyperventilate.

They took her. They took her Hellcat. They even took her smokes.

And she'd kill a baby for a cigarette right now.

She looks around her cell. Looks for things that aren't simply part of the room.

Speaker. Three mattresses. A metal pot to piss and shit in. And a standing faucet coupled to a sink.

Faucet means pipes.

That she can work with.

"Mahalo, MacGuyver."

Athena checks the pisspot. Smells it. Makes sure it's clean. From the size and weight, it should be able to hold a couple gallons. Enough to last her a bit if they shut her off. She fills it with cold water from the tap. Sets it back down.

She tests the weight threshold of the sink. Pushes down then pulls up on it. Ideally, she can snap the basin off then get at the heavier metals of the water-carrying pipes. Maybe even grind a chunk down by scraping it against the floor. Tie a sharpened shard to the pipe with a strip of cloth from one of the mattress. If the point's sharp enough, it'll be a fine weapon.

Then she can maybe crack the glass. Spark plug would be better. Get some ceramic piece and then...

What?

Fuck is she supposed to do here?

To hell with the door. She should look for rivets in the floor. See if she can pry a few loose and lift a metal plate.

Bennett cuts out. An odd, high, giddy voice cuts in. "Don't do that, Mommy." The voice titters.

Athena stops. Sneers. Her eyes find a tiny camera in the corner opposite the speaker.

The high giddy voice says, "Yes." More giggles. "I think you should stop all that goofiness and come have a martini with me. How about it?"

Athena licks her lips. "I want my smokes and my car." She spits. "And my guns."

"Oh, Mommy. I'm really not sure that that's the best idea." The voice chuckles. Hums.

Athena's door unlocks. The human-but-not guard waits in the hallway. Its face is stitched together in patches. Leathery under the brown jumpsuit it wears. It has a black cheek. Yellow lips. White forehead. Some rotten mishmash of races and genders.

She notices that one of its legs is longer than the other.

The gimpy thing waves her toward the hallway.

Athena glances over her shoulder at the camera. Follows a heartbeat later.

The gimp leads her down the hallway.

It's all tight. Cells against cells.

She makes an effort to check every window. Look for Mark. Michelle. Even the goons. Just to give her some idea about where she sits in the hierarchy. She doesn't catch much more than glimpses.

Quick flashes of huddled figures. Stitched together like the gimp.

Shit's further fucked the farther she walks.

Cobbled-together humans give way to masses of flesh. In seemingly random configurations. People-cows with ten udders. A man with fingers stitched into his cheeks that waggle. All of em mewling and screaming. Dripping and crying out in voices no living thing should be able to make.

Like that goddamn noise on the radio.

Snorts. Gobbling. The odd groan of satisfaction.

Athena frowns at the idea of some mad shit like this running around outside.

The hallway leads to a wider area. A junction that splits four ways. The left and right corridors show more cells. The junction itself doubles as a dining hall. One with more stitched together people whose parts don't match. More fiends in brown jumpsuits.

Beyond that the hall becomes...decorative.

Metal walls adorned with garland. Christmas decorations. Photographs and paintings inside garish framed photos of "Doc Frankie." This lanky man in a white lab coat and bright red high heels.

One photo shows him giving a thumbs-up to the camera. Behind is a cow with a dozen extra fat udders affixed surgically. Staples in view. Next is a baby with added skulls but one face. A man with four legs and six arms in some utterly screwed centipede formation.

All with Doc Frankie giving a thumbs-up.

Basically the most nauseating selfies ever.

The paintings, though. These oil things.

They show him as being a stalwart leader. Billowing lab coat. Curly blond hair with bright blue eyes. A chin cut from stone.

And lingerie and red high heels.

One weird presidential portrait.

Athena furrows her brow at the mad bullshit around her.

Perry Como bursts from the facility's speakers. "Papa Loves Mambo."

The gimp prods her to continue. Into the expansive, white tiled room at the end of the decorated hall. Where there're staircases on each side. Luxurious marble steps that curl up to a second floor whose horrors and decadence can only be guessed at.

Between the staircases sits a lanky pale man in a white lab coat on a red couch. His head a wild shock of curly blond hair. Man in his mid to late fifties. His nails red to match his high heels. Teeth yellow and grinning around whatever gummy red lipstick he used on his lips.

He gives Athena an enthusiastic thumbs-up. Says, "I had them make this for me." He waves his hands around at the metal and rock and marble. "I'm Doctor Frankie West." He clicks a button on a laser pointer-sized contraption. A pink neon sign above the sofa bursts into brilliance. It reads "The Doctor" in cursive.

He stands. Shows off his midsection and an erection that looks like an elephant's trunk barely contained by black panties. Does a little dance to Como. Shakes his ass.

Athena grunts.

She thinks, *This's all gotten to be terminally weird.*

But she doesn't say a damn thing.

Doc Frankie looks down at his dick. Slaps an over-dramatized hand over his mouth in a painfully feigned expression of *Uh-Oh.* Then he shrugs. "When you're skilled with a scalpel, I say, why not?" He snaps his fingers. Points to Athena. "Ah."

Athena looks around the room for a quick way to kill everyone *and* herself. Backs up. Maybe kite the fiend. They don't seem too bright. Curb stomp it on the stairs...

Doc Frankie shakes his head. "No. No. That would be a rude." He flaps his hands. "And I am very curious about you. I think you're quite special." He approaches the gimp. "Alas, I don't know where you've been, Mommy. All these years. I don't know where you've been." He unfastens the gimp's leather assflap. Pushes the stiched-together thing's head forward a bit so it's leaning over. Pulls his elephant trunk of a cock out. Starts humping.

The gimp does nothing.

Athena realizes that her hopeful theory about mankind not having quickly degraded is a pipedream at best.

We're all fucked. Doomed. Twisted.

Doc Frankie taps the gimp's back. Giggles. "I'm not *gay,* if that's what you're thinking." He snorts. "Though options are limited." He chuckles. "I made these things, so I trust them. I know they're clean." Frankie humps a bit harder. Shivers. Tucks himself back in. "Two pump chump, what can I say?" He grins and giggles. He sniffs. Snaps his fingers at Athena again. "*You*, though. Talk about trust. I don't trust you at all. If family members can't trust each other, that's just *awful*."

Athena stares at him. She flexes her fingers but she's wary of making a fist in case that's what sets the gimp-thing off. Some sign of potential violence on her part.

Though the weird freak did just take a load of sperm in the pants without any emotion or reticence at all, so...

Probably safe to say anything short of a gunshot and the gimps won't blink.

Actually, it doesn't seem like they blink anyway.

She watches Doc Frankie.

His lanky ass meanders its way back to the sofa. He scratches himself while he walks. Some sticky bits clinging to the fabric of his lacy black underoos.

Doc Frankie flops down dramatically. Stretches out. Wraps one heeled foot over the other. Props his head up with his hand.

Athena notices how goddamn *hairless* the guy's body is. Perfectly smooth. Like an intensely perverse baby. Or a psychotic, in-shape cherub. Which's the opposite of other male..."survivors"—or whatever the fuck they should be called. Most guys give up on shaving entirely.

Not Doc Frankie. Apparently, he's very *particular* about some things.

He looks Athena up and down. "You don't say much, do you?"

Her upper lip twitches. The start of a sneer.

Athena would like to slit this weird fucker's throat. Toss him on a slab. Kick down against his neck till the wound splits and the vertebrae snap so she can look down into his esophageal hole and maybe take a hot shit in it.

But she's gonna need her Buck knife back before that can happen.

She growls. "I want my smokes and my car."

Doctor Frankie licks his lips. Grins. "What about the man and the cow?" He plays around at his lab coat pockets. Produces a pack of American Spirits. A Bic. He flips both from hand to hand like a poker dealer prepping for a round at the table.

He flips em from his wrists so they slide across the floor and stop at Athena's feet.

She dips her knees to retrieve em.

Doctor Frankie grunts. Smiles.

Athena grabs her smokes and her black and white lighter. She's careful not to bend over too far. At least not as far as the weird patched-together thing.

Doctor Frankie whistles all the same. "You've stayed in shape. As a road runner, I mean. Especially as a female." His hand hovers over his belly. "They get fat and stupid. All that time spent behind the wheel and no exercise."

Athena lights her cigarette. Cocks an eye at Doc Frankie. "Some do."

Doc Frankie giggles. "And there again. This weird economy of words. 'Some do.' What am I supposed to infer from that?" His tongue wags outside his mouth. "You're one of the old ones." He jumps from the couch. "Too late to have a baby, but would you protect one?"

He snaps his fingers. Twice. Two screens descend from the marble ceiling on metal cabling. Both show a bobbling view.

"The vision from my bone machines. One screen for each ocular unit." He nods to Athena. "Same brilliant design that got you."

Athena smokes. Her eyes flit between the screens.

*Nobody* has this kind of technology anymore. Not functioning, anyway. Most ends up like all the garbage at the Iron Cross camp. Busted relics. Yet everything at Frankie's is shiny. Pristine.

And the robot that plucked up the Hellcat...

Athena gets robotics. She can't build one herself, but she

understands the enormous amount of work that goes into it from an engineering perspective. There's the body. All those components. Metal. Electronics. Cabling. Power supply. Then programming the software or an artificial intelligence to run the damn thing.

Shit.

"Terminally weird" doesn't begin to cover it.

Doc Frankie points to the screens. Says, "See?" The camera gets closer and closer on a silver Toyota Corolla. Its trunk tethered down by bungie ropes. "This is the skulls' view. My chrome bone machines. They'll snatch the metal of the car. Return it to me. Then keep clearing the highways." He giggles. Nods. "These idiots took seventy-one south out of Cleveland." He hums. "There's a driver and a cow."

Athena grunts.

Doc Frankie arches his eyebrows. "Why do I want them? Glad you asked." He straightens his lab coat. "I would like to pinpoint exactly *which* forms of cancer metastasize the germ. Which forms of cancer are beneficial. Then figure out if those strains of cancer are treatable." He taps his chin. "And the breeding. Yes, the breeding." He smiles. "Sex will always be fun. Well, for some of us. But mostly it's lost its charm, huh?" He nods at the screen. "Babies—*healthy* babies—are hard to come by. They're all gone. But I need healthy babies for the experiments that might lead to a cure. I don't think I'm too far off at this point." He smiles. "I've been at this for a *looooong* time."

Athena watches in first-person as the chrome bone machine lifts the Corolla. Shakes its contents. Black cables from off-screen worm their way into the cab. The backseat. Dig the car's inhabitants out.

The man. The driver. He screams. The cables shove him down into the rib cage of Frankie's chrome bone machine.

Doctor Frankie nods. "For science, of course."

Athena stares.

The bone machine dangles the pregnant woman. Holds her by the ankle. Scans her. Readouts on the screen say her blood type is A-pos. Ethnicity: Black. Eyes a mutant blue.

The baby in her belly: Germ-free.

But.

Cancerous.

A tiny brain tumor.

Doctor Frankie clicks another button on his remote.

Athena doesn't react as the big chrome bone machine crushes the woman in its fist. Blood drizzles between its fingers. The remains of flesh drip down the screen.

The man in the ribcage screams. "No. *No.*"

He cries and weeps and the microphones collect his audible grief.

Athena turns. Faces Doc Frankie. "I want my car."

Frankie flaps his hands at the screens. "Nothing? Really?" He stalks forward. Turns to her. Bows at the waist. "*Nothing?*"

Athena ashes her cigarette. Growls again. "I want my car."

"Wow." Doctor Frankie shakes his head. "Just—" he wrings his hands. Lab coat fluttering against nothing "—wow." Frankie's heels click against the tile. He circles Athena. He scratches his nose. "I...admit that you've thrown me for a loop, Mommy. You've turned into a mean, unfeeling woman."

Athena's eyes become wary slits.

Doc Frankie crosses his arms. Licks his red lips. "If it's not too much to ask, can you please *fucking say something*, Mommy?" He stomps his heels into the tile.

Her upper lip twitches. She takes a final drag off her cigarette. Stomps the butt with her boot. "I want my car."

Doctor Frankie lunges at her. Presses his fingers into Athena's scalp. Her jaw. "Ahhhhh. Say '*Ahhhhh*,' you bitch.»

She fights. Kicks. Growls.

Frankie's fucked up fiend holds her in place.

She fights harder. Lashes out.

And Doctor Frankie doesn't care.

And Doctor Frankie makes a big show of holding Athena's jaw open. He hovers over it. Her maw. Her throat.

He grinds his guts. Curdles snot in his cheeks. Hocks up a mouthful of vile phlegm. Spits. Lets the mucus tumble on a long string of spittle down into Athena's gullet.

Frankie's fiend helps keep her mouth open. One palm pressing her lower jaw. Another set of fingers prying her upper mouth from purchase.

She has to take it.

Frankie grins. "I'm glad you're here." He releases Athena. "I'm really very glad."

So does the fiend.

She drops to her knees. Retches. Dry heaves. Pukes. Bits of dog jerky and whiskey and bile flush free from her stomach as her muscles spasm and send Frankie's nasty gift splashing onto the white tile.

Frankie makes a *tsk-tsk* noise. "*And* you make a mess on the floor. Unbelievable." He drives a red high heel up into her stomach. "Mommy, I am *so* disappointed in you." He shakes his head. Screams. "*Nnngh*. Mommy. Mommy, sorry." Smiles. Laughs. Moans.

Athena pukes again. Falls onto her side. She takes long labored breaths through her nose. Her hands find her ribs. She prods em. Winces.

Frankie's heels *click* and *clack* against the floor as he walks a circle around her prone body. "Now do you have anything to say?"

Athena coughs. Sniffs. She starts to pull herself from the floor. The fiend yanks her to her feet by her leather jack collar. She rolls her tongue around her mouth. Locks her eyes on Frankie. "Thanks for the smokes."

# 11.

Mark and Michelle are tossed into Athena's room a couple hours later. She and he each land with grunts. Then crawl to their beds.

Athena blows smoke. She watches the brother and sister from a corner where she's decided to plant her ass and burn tobacco.

The two settle into something like comfort after whatever nightmarish shit Frankie put em through. The wounds not seemingly physical but mental. Psychological.

She thinks four hours have passed but there's no real way to tell. Just some vague notion.

Athena hasn't seen a fuckin window since they arrived.

Michelle curls up in a ball. She cradles her belly and the baby inside.

Mark doesn't even look at her. He lies on his back and stares at the ceiling.

Michelle shivers.

Athena smokes.

And what the fuck, Dick Clark introduces Frankie Avalon over the radio.

Smoke floats from Athena's nostrils. She still doesn't know where the hell she is.

Mark says, "He was *thorough*. Wanted to know what men I'd been with—"

Michelle pulls herself from sleep. "Shut up."

"And he kept rubbing himself. Like—" Mark shakes his head as he stares at the ceiling "—he gave himself a fucked up monster dick. Kept asking all these weird things about how many men I'd been with. Was I ever with a woman? Had I contracted anything?"

"Shut up. Please shut up."

"And I didn't know what to say. At all. I... I—then he..."

Michelle grabs her brother by the throat. "Shut up. Shut the fuck up or I will goddamn kill you. I swear. I swear on my unborn baby. I will kill you."

Mark's face remains blank. Dumb. A machine of rambling gibberish.

Michelle moans and tosses herself against her mattress.

She and Athena lock eyes for a second.

There's some fatal understanding there. For a moment.

But that moment passes.

And Athena keeps smoking.

Silence for fifteen minutes. A few more pop hits from the fifties.

Athena stands. Strips off her leather jacket. Dunks it in water. Shoves it over the speaker and the camera she knows is buried inside. Holds it in place with her left hand.

Says, "We have to kill him. We have to get outta here."

*I want my car back.*

Mark talks without looking at Athena. "What, precisely, did you have in mind?"

"I think he wants me." She arches her eyebrows.

"Did he—"

Athena shakes her head. "No." She rolls her neck around her shoulder. "If he'd tried to rape me, we wouldn't be talking right now. I'd've gone on a suicide mission to either kill him or get myself killed."

"I'm not sure I believe that at all."

«Point is—"

Mark returns the words with a mockery. "*Point is.*"

"—Point is that everything here works under *his* say-so. The big robots in the field and even his fiends in...wherever we are. Nobody does shit unless Frankie says so."

"Which means what."

Athena scratches her cheek. "He's got a thing about control. We loosen his grip on it, we can fuck him." She lights another cigarette. "Maybe."

Mark sits up. Hisses as his ribs cause him more grief. "I looked around when I was being walked from one surgical area to the next. The, uh, 'fiends?' They're all over. And the cells are magnetically locked. Everything in here is reinforced steel."

Michelle stirs on her dirty mattress. "Shut. *Up.*"

Athena plays with her cigarette. Her bottom lip. She twists it. Taps it. Licks it.

Blinks.

And in a sudden flash it comes to her.

She says, "We need to find those Iron Cross assholes."

Michelle groans.

Athena nods. Flicks the ash from her cigarette. "This's supposed to be what the cocksuckers do. Right? Their whole crazed survivalist thing. The shacks in the woods and the traps from the rampaging highwaymen."

Mark shrugs. "Enemy of my enemy."

"Maybe."

Michelle sniffles. "Don't forget that you killed a lot of em." She chuckles. "And they all wanna kill *you*. Rape *me*... But, boy, let's go make some goddamn friends."

Athena grabs her jacket from the speaker-camera when a fiend pounds on the door and throws it open. The shape doesn't make a sound.

Athena growls.

The fiend lunges for her.

She dodges its fists. Jukes. Pivots under a punch. Brings a fist up into the fiend's midsection. Right around where the liver *should* be. Instead it's like punching a wall. Her knuckles crack. She winces. Worries that she's busted her hand.

The fiend remains silent. Uncaring. It grips Athena around the face. Picks her up by the flesh around her cheeks. Punches her in the gut. Once. Twice. Till her air is gone alongside what fight might be found.

It tosses her onto her mattress.

Surveys the scene.

Turns tail and walks back out.

Athena coughs blood against soft fabric. She locks eyes with Mark. Whispers, "Bullhorn."

* * *

At some point, she falls asleep.

They all do.

Terror and exhaustion and anxiety grinding em down to the marrow.

Athena dreams. Of David. The conversations they had about a baby. Then laughing and smiling and trying for one.

Then the gunshot and the raider that smashed her man's face against the curb.

The guilt of not being fast enough. Not fast enough to kill the motherfuckers before they took David away forever.

Athena's eyes snap open when her body tells her something is nearby.

There are two fiends in the room. Standing. Staring down.

Athena goes for her gun. But of course her pistol's gone.

It's just muscle memory.

Doctor Frankie interrupts Pat Boone over the speaker system. His weird lilting voice cuts into "Ain't That a Shame." Frankie says, "Goooood *morning*, patients. Visitors. Tourists. *Participants*. Annnnd...Mommy. As usual, we have a wonderful breakfast in store. A whole, whole lot of protein. Gruel. Pan-fried locust. Possum grits. And, y'know, my current favorite: Something goddamn strange that we pulled from Lake Erie." There's the sound of lips smacking. Then laughing. "I have no idea what it is, but it's tasty."

Athena lifts her eyebrows. Tries to think of areas along Lake Erie they could conceivably be. Shit that's industrial. Not insanely far from Mercer. Maybe a hundred-mile range.

So...

Cleveland and... Cleveland.

That's the only place that pops into her mind.

Old steel town with equally old buildings.

Could be a candidate.

She starts to think they might be in a basement.

Some expansive underground area of Cleveland.

Could explain the tight spaces and all the damn metal.

Frankie also said he had "them" build shit for him, though.

Ah. Fuck.

Athena stands. Grabs her coat. The leather still damp from before. She lights a cigarette.

Pat Boone fills the speakers again.

Mark and Michelle awake. The corners of their mouths drawn down into frowns. Disappointment. Like they thought they were gonna get good presents for Christmas instead of stockings full of shit.

Tough break.

Athena, Mark and Michelle follow the fiends. Their boots clatter against steel floors. Fluorescent lights buzz over their heads. Long, bright angry insects.

The fiends lead the trio to the mess hall at the intersection. A shiny high school cafeteria. Picnic tables made of metal. Fiends guarding all the entrances and exits. No windows as usual, but another cobbled-together creature behind a counter. Waiting.

Iron Cross goons stand in line. The lunch lady fiend—he... she...it in a chef's apron that has a smiley face and a spatula on it and yellow rubber gloves—slaps slop that *might* be edible onto trays for em.

When they check over their shoulders and see Athena, they forget their food. Stare. Eyeballs full of hate. Grub on their trays steaming but uncared for.

There's about thirty of em. Varying ages. Most in their late twenties or early thirties. No single race dominates the group. A mix of white and black and Hispanic and Asian. The unifying feature is that damn Iron Cross tattoo.

Which makes Athena an "other."

She squints back. Realizes this *is* just like high school again.

Only the bastard Bullhorn takes her arrival in stride. He sees her, sure. Licks his lips and smiles. But doesn't bother with the staring or the posturing.

He carries his tray of unrecognizable "breakfast" and finds a seat for himself. Then digs in. Noisily. With a flimsy spork.

Whatever he's eating is grey. Drippy.

That doesn't stop him.

The goons lose their interest her. Turn back in their place in the line.

Athena, Mark and Michelle take their own spots. Get handed beige plastic trays by a fiend wearing another apron and yellow rubber gloves.

Michelle doesn't say anything as the lunch lady fiend fills her tray.

Neither does Mark.

The siblings carry their crap to the far side of the junction, where there's a spare table. They ignore Athena completely.

Which's fine by her.

The lunch lady fiend plops a fried locust on her tray. Then gruel. Then a meaty chunk of whatever it was Frankie raved about.

Athena walks with her feast and finds Bullhorn. Sits across from him. Studies all the strangeness on her tray.

She has no desire to test the locust. This fat thing the size of an ear of corn. For some reason, she trusts the watery gruel at the center of her tray the most. But the meaty chunk to the right rouses a curiosity in her.

At first blush, she thinks it resembles a cut of bass steak. White meat with grey and black scales. If they're close to Lake Erie, that might make some sense. Except all the nuke plants went to shit. And even Frankie didn't know what his fishers dragged in.

Athena stabs the fish steak with her own flimsy spork.

The scales on it open up. Become a mouth. A dozen mouths. With teeth in a ring around her breakfast.

Food screams.

Other people's trays ignite with sound. Scream and squeal.

And then everyone's fishy food hurls itself from their tables.

Scurries along the floor to get out.

The fiends stomp after the speedy fish steaks. One has a flamethrower on its back.

Bullhorn sighs. Keeps eating. "My own goons can't remember if you don't pike the nervous system at the center of a piece of Erie Whale Eel, well, it goes all sideways."

Athena eyeballs him. Without the megaphone, he sounds somber and almost reasonable.

Almost.

She sips her salty grey gruel. "This ain't new to you."

Bullhorn shrugs. "Nothing is new. Hell, I only sit here cuz the microphones can't hear me from this spot." He cracks off part of the fried locust. A chunk of the thorax. Stuffs congealed protein into his mouth. "I've been here before." He plucks a long tough strand of chitin from his mouth and tosses it aside. "My smile... It was just for you, Hellcat. You have no idea what you're in for." He grins. "You awful fuckin cunt."

Athena shrugs in response. "This coming from a guy with... How many cars were in reserve? That goddamn lynching party of yours coming after me? Trying and failing to catch a Hellcat?

With one woman at the wheel and a .45 1911?" She jabs a finger at Bullhorn. "If you think—"

A goon at a different table attacks a fiend. Slams his plastic tray into the throat of one of the things. Sweat pours from his tattooed forehead. He lifts his hands and the cafeteria is filled with cheers of anarchy from the others.

Athena's gaze snaps to Mark and Michelle.

The two sit and watch and do nothing except move their own food out of the way of chaos.

Goons swarm the nearest fiends. When their trays break, they snap up the sharp shards and drive those shards into the faces and necks of the fiends. *Stab stab stab.*

And the fiends don't give much of a shit.

But when the flesh tears, it gives Athena a rotten glimpse at what the hulking freaks really are: machines covered in the stitched-together flesh of Doc Frankie's former coworkers. Or whoever happened to be around at the time.

Convenient.

She sees chrome skeletons under the bleeding flesh.

Bullhorn keeps eating.

Athena decides the same as chaos envelopes the scene.

Goons run mad on the fiends. They use the weapons they have: plastic tray tables. Sporks.

Athena ignores the maelstrom. Best she can. Stuffs grey calories into her face.

Till a fiend approaches Mark and Michelle.

Bullhorn shakes his head. "Don't do it. Those things don't bleed like you and me."

When the fiend grabs Mark and Michelle around their faces, she loses it. Stands. Snaps a nearby plastic tray over the edge of a metal picnic table. Comes away with a nice sharp blade that fits in her calloused hands like a shiv.

It'll do.

Athena runs low. Shouts, "They're mine." Rushes toward the back of the fiend threatening Mark and Michelle. She jumps from the seat of a picnic table to the wretched thing's back. Instead of stabbing at the fiend's neck, she slices. Grabs the underside of the stitched-together beast's chin. Cuts from ear to ear.

There's a cavernous wound, but no tell of pain.

Just darkness between the flesh and the chrome.

The fiend reaches to its back. Goes after Athena like she's an itch it can't quite scratch. It strains to grab her thigh. Can't tear her off. Tries for her calves then finds enough of a grip to rip her away.

All the while, Athena roars. Pure guttural animal noises.

Till the fiend pins her on a picnic table. A hand around her throat.

A hand that squeezes and cuts off the oxygen.

Athena's face burns red. Then purple. She growls. Slices the strip of plastic across the fiend's face. Loosens some skin there so it falls away from the machine's bones like a *delightful* flaky fuckin pastry.

No meat. Just air.

She feels around herself.

For something.

Anything.

She locks her fingers around a cylindrical object.

A cup of water.

That something.

That anything.

She shoves it into the hole she made in the flesh.

Punches up so the container breaks in its neck hole and her knuckles split.

She hears liquid splash.

The fiend stops. Shakes. Jitters. Humps the air as sparks light up inside it.

Then pitches backward. Drops. Dead. On the ground.

Athena rubs her throat. Kicks herself away. Stands.

And Doc Frankie bursts onto the scene. Panting. He points around. "Stop. *Stop.*" A couple more fiends flow in behind him. His high heels are pristine but his makeup runs. All that red down his chin. Mascara down his cheeks.

He's been up to something.

Frankie shouts. "What is *wrong* with you people?" He flaps his hands. A bird that can't take off. "I mean. *Jesus.* Really. Really? A perfectly fine breakfast. And now it's all gone to crap." He points to Athena. "And *you.* You killed Joe. I can't believe you killed Joe. *Joe* of all people. He was my best wingman."

Athena blinks. Pants. Sweat rolls from her brow. She shakes it off and runs a hand through her close-cropped hair to get the rest clear of liquid.

Frankie pinches the bridge of his nose. "You try to do something nice and, well, what do you get?" He throws his arms up. "A whole lotta nothing. I hope you're all happy." He snaps his fingers. Points around. "Did any of you get the chance to taste the Erie Whale Eel? I just learned what it was."

Bullhorn nods. "Yeah. Real good."

Frankie smiles. Points to Bullhorn. "You know, you see, uhh—" Frankie chuckles. "It's important that a man can eat well. Properly prepared food is critically important to a civilized society. *That* man—" he gestures to Bullhorn "—he knows this. He *knows* it."

Athena cocks an eye. Confused.

Ready to throw a punch, as always, but totally lost.

Without direction.

The only thing Doctor Frankie managed to do was confuse the shit outta everyone. Goons and Athena combined.

The fiends don't attack anyone. They don't even take retribution.

Two pick up the body of the fiend Athena downed. They carry it out of the cafeteria. Toward Frankie's mansion.

The others meander back to their places. Hulking guards in brown jumpsuits. They stand at attention and pay no mind to the Iron Cross that pick themselves up. Look around. Then decide they might as well eat what remains of their food.

And Frankie just...walks away. Saunters down a corridor Athena hasn't visited yet.

She's still breathing heavy. Blood on her face. Split lip. Internal injuries she'll deal with later. Maybe have Mark look at. She drops her plastic shiv. Ready for the next round. Even though there ain't one to be had.

She looks to Mark and Michelle. Nods.

They nod back.

Happy to...

Well, not happy to be here, but happy to be in one piece.

They eat their fuckin breakfast.

Athena drops back onto the bench of her picnic table. Continues to suck gruel.

Bullhorn shakes his head at her again. "Told you not to do it, but you did it anyway. I guess there's something to be said for that." He grins. "So what'd you learn?"

Athena squints.

Bullhorn sighs. Tosses his spork down. "What'd you *learn*, Hellcat."

Athena says, «Robot plus liquid equals dead robot.»

Bullhorn cocks a brown eye at her. "What you should've learned is the true definition of insanity." He stares at his food. "My own goons might be loony, but at least they ain't insane." Bullhorn raises his spork. A chunk of grey meat at the end. "Frankie is *actually crazy*."

"Right, but he—"

"He don't nothing. I know where your thinking is headed."

Athena grunts. Lifts her tray so she can lick it. Not much left. So she breaks a leg off the locust.

Bullhorn squints. "Yeah. You think there's some logic at work here. There ain't." He flips his spork down. "Warlords. My bosses. Me. The goons. Again, maybe psychos on the road, but there's an internal logic. Nothing along those lines for Frankie." He sniffs. "You ever even *heard* of shit like Frankie's? This science fiction craziness. Robots and stuff. What I heard is he was some child genius who went bonkers. Went to MIT or whatever when he was like a little kid. That kinda thing. A master of robotics and theoretical energy production who makes monsters for himself since there's nobody else around."

"So—"

Bullhorn holds up a finger. "Genius or not, Frankie didn't have cameras last time I was here. They ushered me in. I waited a day. Then told one of the fiends I was due to be released."

Athena chews locust leg. "And they just let you out."

Bullhorn shrugs. "They're automatons. They don't *think*. They're just machines inside skin. I walked from one line to the other. Turned around. There're a lot fewer bodies now, but, I mean... You've seen Frankie hump one right? Fuckin weirdo does it every couple hours. Thinks people wanna watch."

He shivers.

Athena drops the locust leg. Doesn't have much stomach for it right now. Better to let the gruel settle. "If you got out before, what're you thinking now?"

Bullhorn groans. Looks around. Makes sure nobody's paying attention to him. Whispers, a voice that's gargled gravel, "I'm tired, Hellcat. Done this kinda shit for ten years already. Not much future in it." He stiffens. Sits up. Talks normal. "Well, uh... If I get you to *submit*, that'd be something, huh? Buy my way out." Bullhorn grins. "A Hellcat all for Frankie."

Athena glowers. "I'll kill every one of you motherfuckers."

Bullhorn sucks his teeth. "You'll *try*. And what about your charges if you take the hero exit?" He points to Mark and Michelle. "The fag and the cow? What happens to them?" Bullhorn bounces. Plays with the cloth around his crotch. "Frankie got one thing right with that elephant cock. Teaches bitches a lesson."

The goons cheer.

She gets it. Him back in microphone range away from the table.

Bullhorn locks his eyes on Athena. "To be honest, honey, the scariest thing you can do to any of us here is a wet dream." The Iron Cross preacher having a good laugh with it cuz everyone can hear. All his goons. He elbows one at a table. Points. "Can you imagine that crazy bitch piloting a bone machine? Or, fuck, what's it... What's Frankie onto now? Oh, oh. An *Eviscerator Suit*." Bullhorn rubs his chin.

Stares at Athena again.

Bullhorn nods. Says, "Yeah, that'd be a helluva thing. Getting your hands on one of those."

Athena pulls a confused face.

She doesn't know what an "Eviscerator Suit" is.

Just knows she *wants* one.

# 12.

Fiends take Mark and Michelle again. Off to whatever weird perversions await em in Frankie's fucked up fun house. None of which Michelle will talk about.

Ever, maybe. But definitely not right now.

Athena stews. Smokes. Processes that whole scene with Bullhorn and the goons in the cafeteria. She knows more than she did, but it ain't enough.

What she'd love to know is just *how many* goddamn fiends there are. She's never seen more than ten together at once.

And she needs a floorplan. A map.

Athena starts a rough sketch of one in her head.

If she makes a right out her door and down the hallway, she ends up at the cafeteria. The cafeteria itself sits at a four-way intersection. She keeps going straight, she ends up in Frankie's manse. Which sucks ass. So she's curious about the end of her hallway and what else is in the other corridors.

Lotta real estate.

Frankie's voice flutters over the speakers. Interrupts the Fontane Sisters' "Hearts of Stone." His voice chirps. "I would like to invite everyone to the auditorium. *Sooooo* move those healthy, er... Shake those butts. Sexy-like. If there's one nice thing about the end of the world, it's that there isn't enough food for folks to stay fat."

Not a true statement. If someone was so inclined, they could gorge on preserved food if they had the rations.

Doesn't matter at all.

Athena plies her ass from her bed. Stands. Straps her leather jacket back on. Her armor. Cigarette between her lips. Smoke snakes over her shoulder. She awaits the fiend at her door.

It stomps in. This one a woman from the upper lip to forehead. Not the *same* woman, but female anyway.

The thing motions for her to exit her cell.

Athena does and finally takes the time to check behind her and count all the doors as she walks forward.

She counts twenty doors on each side of her corridor. Forty rooms. Given the industrial nature of the place, feels safe to assume it's the same in each corridor. Which means one hundred-twenty rooms. And if there's a fiend for every room... Are there one hundred-twenty fiends?

Athena cocks her head. Takes a pull from her cigarette.

Maybe not. Doesn't need to be that many.

Frankie moves his prisoners around at different times. Weren't the goons there in the cafeteria before Athena and Mark and Michelle? Yeah.

Plus, half the cells are filled with those weird flesh-things.

Yeah. So there's a chance it's just an *illusion* of numbers. Of power.

Athena blows smoke through her nose. Mutters, "On the other hand, he's fuckin goddamn *crazybrains* and those bone machines are no joke."

The fiends stop her at the cafeteria. Nudges her to the right. A new corridor and a new direction.

Okay.

She watches the metal doors. Counts em. Comes up with forty.

That gives her a place to start at least. Confirmation.

The hall opens into a theater. Row after row. Then a big fat empty stage. The floor there made from white pine. Perfectly waxed. Behind all that's a massive screen.

As with the cafeteria, goons arrive before Athena does. They occupy the three front-most rows. Bullhorn's at the center, first row.

She sits a bit farther back. Midway in the theater. Plants her ass. Wonders for a brief second is there's a delicacy like popcorn involved.

Butter. Salt.

Holy shit, there is.

A fiend sticks a red AMC bucket of popcorn between Athena's mitts. It's hot and smells...wonderful.

She grabs a handful. Doesn't remember when the fuck she last had fresh popcorn. Salty with all that shitty plastic butter and everything.

Athena chows down. She doesn't give much of a fuck what's going on in that moment. Just goddamn. *Hot popcorn.*

She tries to remember the last movie she saw, too. Thinks about it for a minute. Two. Gives up. She chews. Enjoys the sound and the crunching and even those stupid brown husk things that get stuck between your teeth and your gums.

The lights in the theater space dim. The screen brightens. Words fade in. That weird pink cursive script like the neon shit in Frankie's mansion: "The Doctor Presents..."

Athena cocks an eye. Her chewing slows. She frowns.

Frankie appears on stage. He walks into the bright lights. Hands on his hips. He's...got this black wide-brim hat on that covers a wig of scraggly brown hair. A dark green overcoat. Maroon scarf.

Athena's eyes go wide. Her brain stutters. Ceases to work.

The ten fiends guarding the theater clap their hands together in a stilted way. Mechanical applause.

Frankie bows. Grins.

The raider goons start to chuckle between themselves. They shrug at each other. Giggle. All except Bullhorn, who keeps his gaze locked on Frankie. One scavenger to the left in the front row stands. Points at Frankie. Says, "What *is* this faggy shit?"

Frankie frowns at the noisy goon.

Athena sees him reach into a pocket. Probably after that remote of his.

The fiend nearest the goon snaps its hand out. Wraps its fingers around his skull. Then it just squeezes. The *sound* of the bones cracking. The brain squishing. The eyes popping. The gore that slaps against the floor like chunky soup.

That goddamn noise.

It shuts the goons up.

The fiend releases the body. The carcass slumps to the ground. Still spurting. The fiend snatches it up. Takes it back down the corridor. A river of blood in its wake.

Frankie claps his hands together. A shot going off in the silent theater.

It makes the goons jump in their seats.

Which gets Frankie's smile going.

He holds his hands out and begins his one-man performance of "My Fair Lady."

Athena munches her popcorn.

The goons sit in rapt silence.

And Frankie's voice fills the theater.

He's actually not a bad singer at all.

When the show ends. And Frankie looks off to the side. And mutters Professor Higgins' final line: "Eliza, where the devil are my slippers?" Bullhorn stands and applauds. The other goons follow his lead.

Frankie takes a bow. Then another. He kisses his hands and waves to the crowd. He looks up from his final bow. Stares at Athena—the only one not giving him his apparently-due praise.

He straightens on stage. His lips form a mocking pout. His hands find their places at his hips. He shouts, "Nothing from you, Mommy?" He rubs his forehead. "Wasn't it good enough for you?"

Athena grinds handful of popcorn down between her teeth. She sniffs. Puts the mostly-empty AMC bucket on the ground. Lights a cigarette and blows the smoke toward the ceiling. "I want my car."

Frankie shoots her a curt smile. "Why don't you come on *down*, hm?"

Athena squints. Smokes. Every ounce of her considerable self-respect urges her to scream, "Go to hell, you weird ratfucker." But she doesn't. Cuz now he's got his eye on her. And if she does what she'd do in any other goddamn situation, the fiends'll be all over her. Then they'll either do something strange to her or they'll kill her.

Which isn't how Athena plans to let any of this play out.

She's the only one who gets to decide how and when and where she dies.

So she stands with a grunt. Takes a clue from Bullhorn's begrudging appeasement of the mad doctor. Walks to the steps and the aisle down.

The goons watch her. Stare.

Athena finds Bullhorn's eyes. The Iron Cross mouthpiece is cold. Expressionless.

Frankie flags her onward. "Let's go, let's go. It won't hurt, I promise. Join me on stage here." He dangles a fresh pack of her American Spirit cigarettes. "It's really where you should be, Mommy. Right up here with me."

Athena climbs up. Blinks against the sudden brightness of the stage lights. The heat. She takes her uneasy place next to Frankie. Waits at his right side.

Frankie leans close to Athena's ear. His voice more a reptilian hiss than human speech. "Let's do something *together*. Families are supposed to do things together." He looks out to the audience. Clears his through. "Gentlemen, if you'd be so kind—" he waves his hand. "Whip em out."

The goons furrow their brows. Glance around at each other. Murmur. "Do what?" They turn to Bullhorn. Who sighs. Groans. Gives a faint nod to his colleagues. He unzips his dungarees. Pulls his dick out.

Frankie dips at the waist. "Thank you." He gestures to the others. "Now now. Don't be shy."

The goons murmur more.

Hell. Maybe this'll be fun. They all wanna get laid. Why not run a train on this cranky broad?

Smiles start to populate their faces. Chuckles drip from their mouths.

They follow Bullhorn's lead.

Athena's breathing gets faster. Her heart beats around her chest like a rabid animal. Her fists clench and unclench and shake. She takes a palsied drag from her cigarette.

Frankie drops his black satin panties. Eliza Doolittle with an elephant dick. "Mommy, your jacket please." He hikes his pale dress up. Ties it off at the waist so he's swinging free. Butt and balls to the wind.

Athena jams the cigarette between her lips. Holds it there. Strips off her leather.

Some of the goons in the audience start to squirm. Tug at their pants.

Bullhorn looks utterly miserable.

"Shirt too," Frankie says.

Athena twitches. Sneers. Hesitates. Then stretches the stained white cotton at the neck of her thermal. Removes it. Careful not to burn it with her still-lit cigarette.

She stands topless. Face contorted by hate. Her stomach feels empty and hollow as she waits for Frankie's next command.

But it ain't for her.

Frankie points to the audience. At a goon on the far right. "Now *you* get on up here." He claps. A sick game show host. "Yeah, get on up here."

The other goons grunt and cheer as the scrawny excited psycho jumps onstage. He grins at Athena. Licks his lips. Tugs himself.

Frankie hands the goon a condom. Arches his eyebrows. "Always use protection, young man. *Always*. Remain vigilant at all costs. We must stay disease-free."

The goon chuckles. "Sure. Sure." He rolls his eyes at the crowd. Grabs the condom. Wraps himself. Starts stomping toward Athena.

Frankie puts a hand up. Stops the goon. "Where are you going, young man?" He looks to Athena. Then back to the goon. Laughs faintly. "Oh...no, no. You're not up here for her. You're up here for *me*."

The goon frowns. "What?"

The good doctor turns his bare ass to the goon. Leans over. "I'm sure you can muster up the courage." He reaches for Athena. Both hands outstretched. His fingers wriggle. His voice drops into a low moan. Then slides up into a child-like plea. "Mommy, I need your milk."

# 13.

This time, it's Mark and Michelle staring up as a totally disturbed Athena reenters their cell. Nobody says anything.

The Hellcat driver's eyes remain slits.

Her brow wrinkled lines of confusion and concern.

She finds her mattress. Sits. Props her knees up. Rests her elbows on em. She lights another cigarette.

Then she just sits there for a while.

A long fuckin while.

She doesn't even smoke.

Just lets the blue wisps of burning tobacco flutter around her. Hate.

It churns in her gut. Her mind. A roiling ocean of hate with black tendrils that curl around every aspect of her being.

"Hate."

She plays with the word in her mouth. Rolls her tongue around it. She breathes it in. Lets it emerge from her throat. A low guttural noise. The first sound she's made in hours. But so quiet that neither Mark nor Michelle stirs from their own wretched slumber.

It's only Athena.

The Hellcat and her hate.

# 14.

Nobody looks at each other during the next mealtime. A deep sense of weird shame permeates the air. Total humiliation for all parties.

The goons hang their heads. Avoid making eye contact. Even with each other. When they pick at their gruel, it's in fits and starts.

Only Bullhorn seems...unfazed.

Athena sits across from him.

They stare at one another between bites. The day's dish being gruel. Some kinda soft rice. And rat.

The rat's all right. Not as flavorful as the Erie Whale Eel.

Bullhorn and Athena don't speak. They don't need to.

They let a sad recognition inflamed by determination hang in the air between em.

Everyone's having a perfectly reasonable and uncomfortable and miserable dining experience till Doc Frankie prances through the room.

Then it's fuckin unbearable.

He hums some Bing Crosby bullshit and tousles the hair of every goon within reach. When he gets to Athena, he caresses her shoulders. Plants a kiss on the crown of her skull. "Mommy dearest."

Athena eats. Doesn't respond.

Frankie skips off down the sole remaining corridor she hasn't seen.

She squints at Bullhorn.

He offers her an almost imperceptible nod.

Athena chews rat. "What's his endgame?"

Bullhorn plucks something from between his teeth. A bit of gristle. "You're looking at it. I think." He shovels more meat into his mouth. "I've been on the road for ten years. Five on my own. Three so far with the Iron Cross—I joined em after this shit. The idea of strength in numbers. And as far as I can tell, the only thing the good doctor was ever missing from this place was a fuckin audience."

Athena cocks an eye. "'This shit?' I thought you said you walked in and out." She snaps her fingers twice. "That the fiends were so stupid you could just dupe em."

Bullhorn takes a deep breath. Leans back. Crosses his arms. "Tell the right lie the right way enough times, it ends up true. To everyone. Even you."

Athena grinds her teeth. Sets her jaw. "You got two years unaccounted."

He waits. Considers it. "Yeah. Two fuckin years."

Athena frowns. Stares at her food. Pushes her tray away. Lights a cigarette.

She offers one to Bullhorn.

The goons ain't blind to the transaction. They're just too

mentally screwed to make much fuss. Struck dumb by the insanity. They watch like idiot children as adults go about their business.

How could two people go through that kind of nightmare and...

Bullhorn accepts her stogie. Leans in so she can light it. He takes a lungful. Breathes smoke. Licks his lips. "You always kinda miss it."

He looks across the crowd at his curious comrades. Gives faint nods to the perplexed.

Letting the prison population know.

Athena does the same to Mark and Michelle. Off in their own corner of the mess, as always. Apparently clueless about what massive, desperate wave just crested.

Can't do much about that.

They'll have to figure it out.

Frankie bounces back into the mess hall. Flanked by fiends. His voice high. "Mommy! Mommy! I have something to show you." He shrieks. Squeals. "You are gonna be *so proud*." He nuzzles his face against her chest.

Athena puts her cigarette out in her gruel. Stands.

Doesn't say anything or act shitty.

Just follows Frankie.

His fiends.

They lead her passed similar cells. All forty of em. Filled with random highwaymen. Interspersed by creatures whose only purpose seems to be to keep skin alive. Flesh livestock.

That way Frankie can keep his fiends pristine with new looks.

The rest of the monsters are stuck mewling behind metal doors.

Athena checks their numbers. Fifty or sixty.

There's a glow ahead.

Frankie dances behind her. His hands occasionally find her legs. The space between her thighs. Her lower back. Her breasts.

All while he giggles and titters and prods her on.

Mommy. Mommy? Mommy! *Mommy.*

Athena shakes herself. A quick shudder.

*This is happening. And you will deal with it.*

She remembers some sex ed advocate telling her that strong women, too, were abused. But that fact didn't take away their strength.

Fuck.

Or was it David.

*Fuck.*

Doesn't matter.

Athena tries to comprehend what she sees and the end of the hall. An industrial area lined by halogen. Blue lights.

A meat factory.

A *nightmare* factory built into whatever rock she's trapped in.

Machines whine and plunge and scrape and screw.

Frankie peels himself away from her thighs. Jumps like a loon. Points to the whole rotten fuckin mess. High heels clicking. Lab coat slapping against the pale shanks of his legs. "Look what I made, Mommy!" His voice loses its excitement. Drops two octaves. So he finally sounds like the man he is. "Look at what I *made*, Mommy. I've dedicated my whole life to it. I wonder what those damn fools at the Jet Propulsion Labs would say to *this.* "

A cavern of machines. Assembly lines without end. Robots twist and insert arms and legs into the shoulders and hips of the metal skeletons under the fiends' flesh. Chrome armatures.

Some slap human flesh against metal. Sew skin from the dead and damned that Frankie's creations strip from the highways.

And the *noise*. The ceaseless *kthunk kthunk kthunk*.

New bone machines—which'll spread across the highways like a plague.

Athena backs away from the cavern.

To the side she sees exoskeletons that could fit around the human form. Hulking chrome armor about ten feet tall behind clear windows. There's a series of bars in front of the open-air cockpit. Guns with heavy barrels on both forearms. Curved knives curl out between the armor's knuckles.

Gotta be what Bullhorn mentioned to her.

Eviscerator Suits.

She needs that.

She wants that.

If it'll get her to the Hellcat...

Frankie crawls around her leather-clad legs. A mewling kitten. He scratches at her. "You don't like what I made?" He cries. "You *don't like what I made?*" Shouts at her. An enraged child.

Athena pats his head. This pathetic curly-haired freak at her ankles. A grown man acting goddamn insane and ridiculous. "It's wonderful." Athena takes a breath. "Mommy is gonna take care of everything."

Frankie reaches up her legs. "You promise?" He growls. "Do you *promise*, Mommy?"

She spies four thin lengths of metal near her. Leftovers on a workbench about the size of rulers.

She lifts Frankie's head to her chest. Lets him nuzzle against her breasts.

She suppresses her urge to shudder and vomit as she silently tucks the metal scrap into the back of her pants and under her shirt.

\* \* \*

Frankie walks Athena back to her cell. His mewling is constant. As is the groping. Hands all over her thighs and stomach and breasts. Like a baby that doesn't have a clue.

At her door, Frankie coos. "Good night, Mommy."

Athena turns to him in the hall. Her lips a straight line. Eyelids twitching.

Frankie waits. Brown eyes big and pleading.

She leans forward. Plants a kiss on Frankie's forehead. "Goodnight."

Frankie coos again. Takes off down the hall.

Athena steps into her cell. A fiend bolts the door.

Mark and Michelle stare at her.

She nods to em. Tells Michelle—who's got the bed next to the wall, which means farthest from the camera, "I sleep there now. Move to my mattress."

Michelle blinks. Looks to Mark.

He stands. Takes his sister's hands. Helps her up and ushers her over to the third bed. Farthest from the wall. Closest to the camera.

Athena plops down.

Mark says, "What was that? The 'Mommy' stuff? What was that?"

She stealthily pulls one of the rulers of metal from the back of her leather pants. Back to the camera. She tucks it up into the long sleeves of her shirt and jacket. So it's against the flesh of her forearm. Then lets a little slip. Starts to grind it at an angle against the metal floor.

"Hey," Mark says. "What *was* that."

Athena stares ahead. Grinds metal.

He reaches for her. Lays a caring hand on her shoulder. Gentle.

She glares at him and he pulls back. Takes a breath.

Mark whispers, "Feeling...disassociated is a normal reaction to trauma."

Athena rotates just her head. Gives him wide eyes. A fake smile.

She nods like a fool. Head bobbling. "You don't say? Trauma." Hisses. Keeps grinding the edges of her scrap. "Huh. Nope. Not trauma."

Mark eyes her. Keeps his distance.

Michelle frowns and caresses her pregnant belly. She gets it. A little. "What're you gonna do?"

Athena grinds. Lights a cigarette. "I'm going to kill them all."

A grim grin crosses Michelle's face. "I was hoping you were gonna say that."

For a heartbeat, Athena sees something in the pregnant woman's eyes. Something that makes her think the brunette might survive all this shit: pure, unfettered hate.

# 15.

Athena meets Bullhorn in the mess hall. Same as always.

Only difference is the dish today's antlion chili.

Foot-long red chitinous legs arc out from the center of her soup bowl between gruel and grits. They stand, pads down, against her lunch tray.

Everyone in the mess looks like they're gonna have a Burroughs breakfast.

Athena slides two of her ground-down metal shivs under her tray. The sharp edges poke out one side. They've got short handles made from strips of mattress cloth and leather she cut from her jacket sleeve.

She stares at him.

Bullhorn chews antlion. Sucks the boiled protein from chitin. Slides his tray next to hers so they're touching. Lifts the edge a little. Sniffs.

Athena flicks her metal.

They slide under his tray.

Bullhorn nods. "*Dos?*"

"Got a candidate. Hope you do too."

Bullhorn grunts.

Athena lights a cigarette. Smokes it while she eats her gruel. Puffs between mouthfuls. Her eyes wander from fiend to fiend. She grabs a palm of gruel.

Bullhorn says, "You got a time? A plan?"

She lifts her eyes from her plate just long enough to meet his. Her blue eyes blink once.

Athena hears a fiend stomp behind her.

She peels away from her bench. Launches herself at its neck. Cuts the flesh. Rips the flesh. Slathers the circuitry with gruel.

The fiend stutters. Sparks. Starts to tumble.

Bullhorn roars. A shiv in each hand.

Athena moves like a mad chimp. A frenzied animal. She flays fiends. Snatches at picnic tables for cups of water she can hurl into their circuitry. Gets a couple down. Mounts another one's back as other move in to secure the area.

Sirens blare. Sound like the old air raid cries. Their wails rise and fall and seem to go on forever.

She growls. Bares her teeth. Cuts into the flailing neck of the fiend she rides and sees a blue glow at the top of the spine.

Guess it's a neural node...thingy. Who the fuck knows. It looks important. Some bright glowy ball that keeps these assholes together the same way a human brainstem does. Circuits and stimuli instead of flesh and fear.

Athena grunts. Severs the connection at the base of the skull by severing the wires with her shiv.

Sparks and electrical arcs splash against her leather. The

machine stops dead and tumbles forward. The force of the impact dents the metal floor.

Athena makes a mental note *not* to be under one of the fiends if it's gonna die.

Bullhorn watches her. Nods in admiration. He screams. "Base of the skull, boys. *Base of the skull.* Use your crazy *for the Iron Cross.*"

Athena shouts with him. "Cut the wires attached to the blue."

Bullhorn screams. "Rip and tear. *Rip and tear.*"

Goons leap around her. Psychotic bullfrogs. United and inspired behind a single, simple cause. One they grab hold of with suicidal glee.

Two or three of em clamp onto a single fiend at the same time. Those with plastic shards slice the flesh in a frenzy. Whoop and howl.

Those without weapons pull on patchwork skin with nothing more than their gloved fingers. They pull away chunks of it. Some bite into the machines' necks. Snap their own teeth in the assault. But it does get em access to the blue nodes. Which they punch and bash with their fists.

One dumb goon tries to chew the node. He does crack part of it.

For his efforts, all the power in the fiend charges through his face. All that juice. It pops his eyeballs. Turns him into a smoky husk.

Mark puts himself between Michelle and the chaos. He pushes her back against the wall.

Michelle lets Athena's metal shiv dangle from her right hand. Her eyes flick from goon to goon and fiend to fiend. If it wasn't for the baby in her belly, she looks like she might want to exact some revenge.

A goon sails through the air in front of Athena's face. Backward. He ain't attacking. A fiend's chucked him away so hard that the back of his head shatters against a metal wall like an overripe watermelon. Brain and bone slide to the floor in ragged chunks.

Frankie stands in the hallway that leads to his mansion. He shrieks. Long and loud and high-pitched. His cries shake the paintings and photos around him. He squints at Athena. "Why? *Why, Mommy?*" Then he roars.

Athena points her blade at him. "Come on over, honey." She sneers. "I'll explain everything."

The mad doctor's eyes go wide. He lifts his remote from his lab coat pocket. "You'll never get this you wretched whore. And without *this*, the doors out don't open." He turns. Scampers. Cackles as he clicks buttons and a massive metal door shuts behind him. Sealing the corridor off.

Well, shit.

A goon squeals as a metal monster tears both of his arms off and beats him to death with em.

Athena ducks the grabbing hands of another fiend. Twists. Rolls away. Under one of the metal tables.

The fiend punches the tabletop. Goes right through it. The broken strips around the hole flay the jigsaw-flesh of its forearm. Farther. All the way up to its shoulder.

She rolls out the other side. Gets to her feet in time to see Bullhorn shiv the back of the fiend's neck.

The machine crumples.

Bullhorn locks eyes with her for a second before moving on to help the goons who're still alive. Which ain't too many. Ten are splattered in various portraits of gore around the lunchroom. But their swarm attacks have been effective. If suicidal.

Three fiends remain.

One of em lunges for Mark. Grips the front of his shirt with a massive gloved hand. Tosses the poor broken bastard like it's nothing.

A small shocked scream escapes Michelle's mouth. But she doesn't cower. She holds the shiv up. Slashes it across the fiend's face.

Athena thinks: *Baby steps, but the brunette's getting there.*

She lunges for the fiend. Hammers the shiv into the back of its neck. Again and again. Till the blue light goes out. The fiend dies.

Michelle scrambles to get outta the way of its heavy carcass.

Athena checks over her shoulder.

Mark wheezes. Coughs blood. He picks himself up from the picnic table he collided with. Groans and limps over the bodies of the ruined goons.

Bullhorn and the seven remaining psychos cheer as they down the final fiend. Its metal body joins the nine others.

Michelle says, "Is that it? Is that all of em?"

Athena looks around. Steps over the bodies and the parts of bodies. If there were more fiends, they'd definitely be trying to kill every human in the room. So it stands to reason...

She nods.

Frankie's voice roars over the speakers. "You *bastards*. You ungrateful *bastards*. After all I've done for you. Wasn't the food good? Did you not enjoy 'My Fair Lady?'" He sighs. Once and loud. "Mommy, I'm disappointed in you the most. I wanted you to be with me. I wanted to build things to show you. I thought you belonged here. And we *were* working well on our trust issues."

A new alarm splits the air. A buzzer.

The blue lights turn red.

There's the harsh crash of metal being thrown against metal.

Every single cell door is thrown open.

The sounds of animals slither down the corridors to the human ears waiting at the lunchroom hub.

Some insane gibbering. And laughter. It echoes. Bounces against the metal walls. They hear the dry heaves of a body that wants to puke. The muttering and snorting of large creatures. Fat fleshy feet slap against the metal under em.

The shapes. Abominations. Black silhouettes against the red glare of the lights. Countless arms and legs. All in the wrong places. All of em trundle along. Take those huge breaths. Giggle and huff.

Bullhorn says, "Flesh can be killed." He snaps his fingers. "Scavenge."

He and the goons pour over the remains of the fiends. They pry apart the bodies of their fallen enemies. Find struts of metal that could become bludgeons or spears. A fiend's upper arm piston becomes a truncheon. One from the monster's lower leg, a baseball bat.

A goon offers one of his metal pikes to Athena. His head bowed. Slightly. In shame. "For the Hellcat." The weapon is two lengths—maybe a machine's femur and tibia—threaded into a T-junction.

Athena takes it. Hefts it. Thing's got decent weight. How the goon broke it or cut it off leaves the length with spear-like tip. It's a fine weapon, under the circumstances. "What's your name?"

"Sherlock." The goon still won't meet her eyes.

He's a black kid younger than the others. "Bullhorn says my name's on account of I'm clever." And he shouldn't remember much. But maybe he remembers some of the ideas and ideals before the germ. At least enough to be ashamed.

Athena watches the encroaching shapes. The mish-mash of insanity lumbering on all sides. She sticks two fingers in Marcus' face. "For them."

Sherlock nods. Looks to Mark and Michelle. Grunts.

Michelle tightens her grip around her shiv. She holds Mark's shoulder. For balance more than anything else. The pregnant woman eyeballs Athena.

And Athena holds her gaze.

Whatever is gonna happen is gonna happen.

Athena wonders if Michelle is ready.

She glances at Mark and sees that he's still looking for a rational explanation. Vision bouncing from goon to Bullhorn to Athena to the dark shapes. But unlike his sister before, he ain't seeking a target.

Sherlock brings back two more pikes.

Athena thrusts one into Michelle's waiting hands.

The second into Mark's hesitant mitts.

She shoves her face into his. "Kill or die, doc."

Bullhorn taps her shoulder. "Incoming, Hellcat."

Athena keeps her eyes on Mark. Glowers. Till the stinking shapes are at the threshold of the lunchroom. Then she turns to em. Pike in hand.

The first one is a pathetic, crawling melted man on his hands and knees. There's too much fatty skin for his bones. It hangs the way curtains do. Loose and draped and dragging along the dirty floor. *Shlorp. Shhhhlorp.* He moans. Giggles. Mouth fulla saliva and no teeth or tongue.

A goon approaches the giggling abomination with his spear readied as others move to cover the other halls. He doesn't seem to consider the giggler too dangerous. He lets it get close before jabbing.

Too close.

The giggler rears back on its knees. Throws its arms out. The jiggly flaps of skin suddenly more like a membranous wall of flesh.

The goon jerks back. Not fast enough.

The giggler wraps itself around the goon. They both thud to the metal floor. A writhing, insane mass.

Athena can see the goon's frenzied attempts to push through the blankets of skin. She can hear his muffled screams. Bones breaking. All amid the lunatic chuckles and chortles the giggler emits.

Bullhorn bashes its head with a heavy rod. There's a splash of red. The giggler's neck snaps to the side. But it won't stop panting. Open mouth drooling. A dumb dog-like smile on its lips.

He hits it again. From the side. A swing meant for a baseball field.

The giggler's jaw flops away. A torrent of clear spit with it.

Bullhorn brings the rod down one more time. Right on the abomination's forehead.

Its skull cracks. Skin splits. Brains become pink and grey paste.

The giggler flops down. A pool of loose meat. But the goon underneath ain't struggling anymore.

Bullhorn doesn't bother checking on his fallen comrade.

Other goons fare better.

Sherlock pins a scuttling monstrosity with his pike. What used to be a woman. Now an emaciated jumble of appendages with stringy hair. Six arms ring its chest. Six more around its belly.

To Athena, the damn thing looks like some fucked up fleshy tree.

Those dozen hands with long nails reach and shriek for Sherlock.

He fights to keep the beast at bay. Just long enough for a second goon to skewer it through the side of the head with his own spear.

Sherlock kicks the corpse off. Roars as he approaches another abomination. Another woman. Covered in pink udders like bloated pustules that leak milk.

Athena rages forward. Her pike up. She runs it through the neck of a creature with no face and three mouths full of teeth. Then another with a wobbly rubbery body. It's face a farm for dozens of human eyes that blink at random and squint and cry.

Behind her, Mark still looks useless. He holds his pike up. Some magic charm he doesn't know how to use. He wields it as a cross. Or some other totem that might keep bad things away with its mere appearance.

Michelle knows better. Acts better.

She stays on offense.

A skinny man who looks as though he's been run through a wringer ambles toward her. Them. His gait is off. Long halting steps. Mark stares at the shape.

Michelle spears it through the face before it gets too close.

Athena is strangely proud that the pregnant woman was able to break through the skull.

It isn't until a small baby-thing wanders toward em that Mark does much at all.

The baby-thing is small enough that it escapes almost everyone's attention. Some sick mutation. Creation. Where three bodies are melted together and act as one. Six pudgy legs. Six pudgy arms.

The baby-thing mewls.

Waddles.

Two feet high. After a few steps, it looks like it's gonna tumble the same as any tot. A short flabby body fighting inertia.

The thing cries out.

Waddles toward Michelle.

No way to tell what it'll do when it gets to her legs.

She gawks. Looks like she can't fathom the reality of this particular abomination.

Marks finally acts.

He shouts as the baby-thing leaps for Michelle's chest and ends up on the edge of his spear. He slams the itty bitty bastard to the floor. Breaks its body against the metal plates. The baby pops. A balloon of dark red paint. Splat and splash and then it's nothing but a smear alongside all the others.

Frankie pants over the speakers. Knowing the elephant-cocked freak, Athena figures he's been jerking it to the carnage up in his manse. He moans. Says, "I can't *believe* you people." He huffs. "Do you have any idea how much time and energy went into my flesh farm?"

Athena wipes the sweat from her brow as she spears what she thinks is the final abomination. A dark-skinned woman with four sets of legs and bellies. Pulsing vulva between every thigh. Stomachs fat with either food or new monsters ready to be birthed into the rotten world.

She jukes a leg that kicks for her face. Stabs the metal through its sole chest. Thinks she hits the heart. Cuz the creature cries out. Stumbles. Tumbles down. Then she makes sure to abort whatever might be growing inside the walking uterus. Jabs the sharp tip of the pike into each belly.

Athena looks for Bullhorn. Finds his dark eyes. The raider stands with his remaining five goons. All of em bloody. Tired.

He nods to her. Jerks his head in the direction of the corridor that leads to the machine room.

Athena follows.

Mark and Michelle move after her.

The ragtag group's footsteps alternate between hard clomps against metal and soft *splortches* as they trod through the blood and guts of battle.

Red lights in the hall gives way to the blue of the industrial room. The ceaseless *kthunk kthunk kthunk* of machines putting together more machines. This incestuous method of creation.

A fraud.

*The* fraud of life. Creation.

Mark and Michelle are struck with awe. The vast expanse carved into the rock. Conveyors and robotic arms. One piece being fit into another. Another. Another.

The bots are still making bone machines. Frankie's highway cleaners.

Athena cocks an eye. Wonders how focused Herr Doktor is on expanding his empire of madness.

Probably pretty fuckin focused.

Far as Athena can tell, there are three degrees of insanity. Her. Goons. Then whatever the fuck Doc Frankie is.

Bullhorn snaps his fingers. Points to a computer terminal.

Sherlock scampers toward it.

Athena scans the industrial area for weapons. Tools. She notices now how the dark grey metal of the rest of the place turns chrome near the factory floor.

Shiny shiny shiny.

Sherlock hammers his keyboard with furious intent.

Frankie's voice on the speakers again: "What are you doing, Mommy?"

Doris Day's flowery and obnoxious and nauseating "Whatever Will Be Will Be" fills the air.

Athena lights a cigarette. Looks left to where the Eviscerator Suits are locked up. Looks right, where there's some kinda storage area staffed by big cargo bins. She didn't see it before. A tad preoccupied by the weird fucker who wanted her tits.

It's another sealed-off section. Heavy metal door with windows.

She approaches the glass. Or plastic. Or whatever. Squints to make out what's inside.

One of the bins reads "HELLCAT" in stamped letters.

Athena pounds a fist against the window. Once. Twice. "That's mine." She stomps toward Sherlock at the console. Points to the door of the storage area. "Open that."

Sherlock offers an exhausted sigh. "Holy shit, it's not like I'm *not trying* here."

Athena growls. She hefts her pike and throws it across the path.

The spear pounds the window and clatters to the ground. Totally ineffectual.

Bullhorn shakes his head. "It's palladium glass. Nothing we can do will crack it."

Athena smokes. Paces. Folds her arms across her chest.

A minute passes. Two.

The machines making machines halt. Conveyors cease. Slow to a chug. Then nothing. The robot arms stop.

A half-constructed bone machine leers from the center of the pit.

The storage area door *shwicks* open.

Athena runs to it. Grabs her big box. Slams it to the ground. Opens the flaps. Finds her .45. Ammo. Mags. Her sawed-off shotgun with the sling attached and a few dozen shells. A couple extra packs of cigarettes. Her Buck knife. Car keys.

The rest she doesn't need. Ain't gonna be sniping anything in here.

Bullhorn and his five goons do the same.

They take what they need from the boxes that designate their vehicles.

Their identities.

That's how she learns their names. The men she shared the most humiliating experience of her life with—and who had to share each other—against their goddamn will.

F250.

Charger.

Mustang.

Impala.

Wrangler.

Athena puffs her American Spirit. "We're just things."

Sherlock cries out: "I got it."

The big door to the Eviscerator Suits *shwicks* open. There are three of em Athena can see. All in a squatting position. Twelve feet tall.

Goons grab their guns and anything else they care about. Which ain't much. Storm back across and into the blue room with the exoskeletons.

Bullhorn steps into one as the others arrive. Pulls himself into its embrace.

He steps up. Plants his ass in the pilot seat. The machine senses him. Locks around him. Spikes along the spine and skull and arms and legs throw themselves through his skin. Some kinda neural interface. Bullhorn screams. His head drops. The Eviscerator holds him aloft.

A heartbeat later he blinks. Up at the room. He says, "It...takes you." He looks away from his goons. To Athena. "It becomes you. Or you become it. One of those." He flexes his fingers. Human and exoskeleton as one. Hulking robotic armor that looks like a chrome bipedal beetle.

Bullhorn smirks. "I could take on an Erie Whale Eel myself."

She smiles back. Reaches for an Eviscerator Suit. "Give to Mommy."

Athena grips the double handrails on either side of the pilot seat. Hauls herself up. Sits. Pulls the barred canopy down. It *clang*s into place. Locks. The suit lights up. Blue LEDs on the shoulders. Elbows. Palms. Knees. Feet.

She slides her arms into the exoskeleton's sockets. Fingers meeting gloves at the end. There's a jolt of intense pain. The needles of neural spikes drive through her skin. Into the muscle. Even into the fiber of her nervous system. Her spine.

Her vision flashes white for a split second.

Then she and the machine are one.

Athena feels it. Her size and weight. The bulk of the Eviscerator.

She's morbidly glad of Frankie's genius.

Bullhorn waves a chrome hand at her. "Feels good, huh Hellcat?"

She nods. "Now let's kill that motherfucker."

It's an apt choice of words.

# 16.

Athena, Bullhorn and Sherlock storm back down the corridor. The heads of the Eviscerators barely low enough to avoid scraping the ceiling. The four remaining goons—plus Mark and Michelle—follow in a rush.

They arrive at the hallway of paintings. All those ridiculous photos of Doc Frankie.

Athena grunts. Raises the guns on the Eviscerator. Sends a thunderstorm of bullets downrange. She doesn't know the exact caliber, but they're big. Maybe 20mm.

And they wreck shit real good.

Explosive rounds will do that.

Dent the metal.

Obliterate Frankie's photos with a vengeance.

Send his visual masturbation into fluttering tatters and flames.

She knows she should worry about ricochets. Metal fragments bouncing away and shooting backward. Maybe killing a goon or Mark or Michelle.

But she doesn't give much of a damn at the moment.

This is too...therapeutic.

Athena's guns run dry. The Eviscerator reloads itself with ammo from some unseen compartment. It tells her, in a digital version of Frankie's voice, that she has two more reloads remaining.

Bullhorn and Sherlock march ahead once the weapons fire stops. They run their robotic fingers along the titanic metal door. Look to each other. Shrug.

They guide the blades between the Eviscerator's knuckles into the gap between the floor and the door. Try to gain some leverage.

Sherlock manages just enough for Bullhorn to slip his fingers under the edge. Hold it up an inch. Two. Enough for Sherlock to grip it as well.

The door groans. Gears in the walls scream out as Bullhorn and Sherlock fight em to get the barrier up. Both men strain. Even their exoskeletons shudder. Powered armor pushed to the extreme.

Something behind em roars. Makes the same broken digital bass note the bone machine did back on the highway.

Athena spins. Raises her guns.

Goons gather at her flanks. Their pikes up.

Frankie pops onto the radio again. He's unusually brief. "Fuuuuuuuuuuuuuuck you, folks!"

Another deep digital note cries out. Then a stomping. Pounding. The high whine and squeal of metal dragged against metal.

Bullhorn and Sherlock grunt. They raise the door. Little by little.

The bone machines are too large to fit inside the hallways, but that doesn't mean Frankie hasn't told his rotten machinery to create something new and ruinous.

Which's what pokes its head around the corner.

Part of a chrome skull. Teeth. No nose. One red eye.

The cyclops cries out. Scuttles into the hall.

It's built like a centipede. Ten feet long. With a dozen arms that terminate in fully articulated hands with spikes for fingers.

Athena grunts. Opens fire.

Explosive rounds tear into the cyclops. Shatter its red eye. It's face. Even blow part of its spine off and sends limbs flying in a spray of sparks and chrome.

Another takes its place. Spiky fingers *click* and *clack* against the ground. Along the walls.

Then there's another. And another.

The cyclops bastards emerge as fast as Frankie's factory can crank em out.

Athena pours the bullets on. Downs two more before her Eviscerator's gotta reload.

A third cyclops rears back. Cries out. Jumps for her.

She snatches it in midair.

Its lower spiked hands curl up. Wrap around the Eviscerator. Around her. It grabs and snaps.

She shouts in pain as its fingers dive into her right thigh and slash the leather that's served her so well. The spikes act like a tiller. They punch into the fat and meat of her. Then open up. Spin. And rend the flesh.

The cyclops chitters. Gurgles.

She screams. Tears in her eyes.

Athena can feel it pulling the blood from her. Draining her.

Frankie laughs over the facility speakers.

She grabs the cyclops's face with her free hand. Crushes its skull and tears it off. Drops the body. Her voice hoarse and strangled, she says, "Fuck you."

Bullhorn yells, "If you're going, go now."

He and Sherlock finally have the door up. But they're shaking. Won't last long. Even with the Eviscerators.

Mark and Michelle run under. As do four goons.

Athena and her Eviscerator limp forward. She turns occasionally to pepper the incoming horde of centipede machines with explosive rounds.

She meets Sherlock's eyes.

Bullhorn's.

He nods.

She ducks under.

The big metal door slams down behind her.

She looks around the vacant entrance to Frankie's mansion. All that marble and wannabe grandiosity. Illusions of importance and grandeur.

And from the locked corridor, the sounds of combat. Violence. Gunfire.

Frankie's voice cackles. Echoes in the empty space.

Athena opens the Eviscerator cockpit. Tries to get to the ground on her feet but topples and lands on one knee. Her blood gushes against the white marble. She groans. Clenches her fists. Squints in an attempt to keep the tears inside her eyelids.

Fails at that.

Mark runs over. Examines the mess of Athena's leg. "Shit." She's lost a lotta blood. He snaps his fingers at a nearby goon. "I need fabric. Give me part of your shirt. A sleeve. Anything."

The goon looks from Mark to Athena. Bites his lip. Doesn't want to, but after seeing her torn apart thigh, he relents. Puts his pike down. Drops his jacket. Tears off the ratty black shirt underneath. Tosses the whole thing to Mark before putting his jacket back on.

Mark drags the shirt along the tip of his spear. Makes a hole. Rips the dark cotton into long strips. Loops those strips and cinches them around Athena's thigh. Tight enough to make her hiss and curse.

He says, "I'm going to need to get a better look at that when I have access to surgical tools."

Athena lights a cigarette. Pants. Nods. Pats Mark's shoulder.

He helps her stand.

She hobbles to the Eviscerator. Eyesight swimming. Grabs her shotgun from the rack next to the pilot's seat. Slings it over her shoulder. Checks her jacket pockets for shells. Feels for the .45 on her hip. Mags in their pouches at her lower back.

Athena turns to face Frankie's couch. The stairs. That bright neon sign.

The goons gawk at their new surroundings.

One of em says, "What the hell kinda place is this?"

Athena breathes smoke. "Frankie's funhouse." She doesn't recognize the music that plays over the speakers now. It's light and dopey and kinda mindless. Could be Lawrence fuckin Welk. "Don't touch nothin."

She listens for more heavy weapons fire from the sealed off corridor. Doesn't hear any. Could mean Bullhorn and Sherlock finished off the cyclops machines. Could mean they're the ones who got dead.

Mark and Michelle and the goons stare at Athena. Like she's supposed to know what to do next.

One of the goons says, "So...we got a plan here?" He shifts his weight from one foot to the other. Anxious. Old revolver in a holster under his left armpit. Spear in his right.

Athena takes a final drag from her American Spirit. Drops

it to the marble. Winces as she lifts her damaged right thigh and grinds the stogie out under a boot heel.

She says, "I have no idea what's in here. This's as far as I ever got. But Frankie's waiting." She tilts her head toward the stairs. "He's here. Somewhere."

The others wait and watch her. Unsteady. Unsure.

Athena grunts. Pulls her Springfield Armory 1911. Limps toward the stairs on the left. She holds the railing as she makes her way up. One painful step at a time.

Mark and Michelle follow her.

The goons take the stairs to the right.

Athena checks the area from side to side. But there's nothing there. Only a door straight ahead. A big wooden one. Dark. Maybe mahogany. It's ornate. Decorated with embossed bones that have a silvery sheen. Cursive writing at the top says, "Home Sweet Home."

She expects the knocker to be maybe a giant dick and balls, but it's not. It's just a chrome ring a few feet above the knob— which she taps her gloved fingers against. Not wanting to grab it with all her might for fear it's wired to electrocute or some other shit.

She tests it. Twists it.

Opens the door.

Raises her .45 and backs away to see what happens. To see if another machine bastard's gonna burst out at em.

Nothing. Zip.

Athena marches in.

Her boots go from clapping against marble to clomping against a hardwood floor. Then thick Persian rugs.

The space is massive. Thirty or forty feet wide. Walls with chrome crown molding set into the wood. The ceiling waits twenty feet above. Crystal chandeliers hang from it. Fifty feet back, a crackling fireplace built into the wall spews warmth.

Bookcases surround it all. Their shelves weighted down by thick volumes and dozens of jars loaded with light green liquid and...fetuses. Body parts. Heads with chunks of neck remaining whose open-eyed nightmarishness watches forever over relics from the old world.

There are dark wooden desks atop which sit degrees from various universities. MIT. CalTech. Cornell. École Polytechnique Fédérale de Lausanne—which Athena can't even pronounce. They're all made out to Dr. Franklin West.

The red sofas feel like velvet. Brown leather armchairs. Art deco lamps made from brass with green shades. Ancient microscopes. Hand-painted globes that still call Russia the USSR.

A goon half-heartedly spins one. Sneers.

The final touch of weirdness to the room is a life-sized. framed portrait of Doc Frankie splayed out on his couch that waits above that big fireplace.

Athena rubs her neck. Thinks, *Cuz of course* that's *there*.

Her eyes flit from object to object. She scans for doors. If this's Frankie's living room, there's gotta be a kitchen. Dining room. Bathroom...

She shudders at the thought of Frankie's bedroom.

The mad doctor's voice pipes up over the speakers again. "Welcome home, Mommy. I don't remember the last time you were here..." He giggles. "I've done a bit of remodeling. So you should definitely be careful."

Athena grunts.

A goon meanders over to the jars and their unpleasant contents. The same one who gave up his shirt to bandage her thigh. He squints. Leans in. Gets his face close to a fetus that's got five eyes randomly placed around its skull and no jaw.

An early experiment, Athena figures.

Before she can remind the goddamn goon not to touch anything, he taps the glass.

The fetus blinks.

The goon jerks back.

Michelle frowns. Holds her belly. Her throat convulses. As though she's fighting to hold back vomit bubbling in her throat. "Oh, God."

One by one, the jarred abominations awake.

Liquid splashes.

Hands with mouths and tails attached swim in tight circles. Fingers stretch. Claw at the glass.

Vacant-eyed heads become aware. Focus on the goon. On Athena. They smile. Perfect smiles with gleaming teeth. The smiles grow into mad cackles.

The goon grimaces. Grabs the fetus jar. Lifts it over his head and smashes it to the ground. He pulls a leg back to kick the itty-bitty bastard.

Before he can, the fetus leaps to its feet. Chitters. Dives to the side. It spins. Pistons itself along on tiny legs. Pitter patter. It's faster and stronger than it has any right being.

It jumps up his leg.

The goon scrambles to grab it. Misses.

The fetus scurries around his back.

He can't...quite...reach it.

Then the damn thing rips his mouth open at the cheek. Pushes his teeth apart. Throws itself down his throat.

He bites down in some sad attempt to catch the fetus, but it's too late.

The goon doubles over. Windpipe choked. Face red. He clutches his stomach. Squeezes it. Either to force the fetus out or to make himself throw up. Which's one and the same.

He stands with a sudden rigidity. Stiff as a board. Hands palsied at his sides.

His stomach expands. The flesh balloons. Pushes outward.

Athena can see the fetus's little hands outlined by pale flesh. Its head. Even its many eyeballs.

And a jaw that opens and closes.

Chews.

The goon screams.

The heads on the shelves continue to cackle.

Skin on the goon's belly splits. Spills blood. Bile.

The fetus reaches a hand out into the air.

Michelle buries her head against Mark's shoulder.

Athena fires twice. Big .45 rounds. The first ruptures the goon's forehead. Puts him outta his misery. The second explodes the tiny body of the fetus.

And the heads just keep on laughing.

The three remaining goons make a move for the jars. Raise their spears.

Athena shouts, "*Stop.*"

Michelle covers her ears. "Why are they laughing." Not a question so much as a helpless plea. Her voice hits a fever pitch. "Why are they *all laughing.*"

Mark wraps his arms around her.

One of the goons points to Michelle. Says, "We're gonna shut em up."

Athena hobbles toward em. "Why? You're playing Frankie's game, you goddamn assholes." She squints at the goons. Eyes move from face to face. "Let em laugh." She snaps her fingers at Michelle. "You gotta suck it up. Find your spine."

Frankie coos over the speakers. "Yessss. Suck it all up."

Athena sighs.

She's feeling pretty goddamn woozy from the blood she's lost. The blood she *keeps* losing cuz the cyclops severed arteries.

Fuck it.

She tucks her .45 into its holster. Winces as she walks to one of Frankie's expensive-looking fancy chairs. Red and more velvet. She hefts it. Bashes it against one of the big desks. Once. Twice. Till it splinters and she can break one of the legs off.

She slices the seat cushion apart. Tears the fabric. Ties it tight around the top of the chair leg. She makes her way toward the fireplace. Lights her torch. Glances up at the painting of Frankie. Meets the eyes there in oil.

Then sets it ablaze.

She shouts, "Keep watching, Frankie."

The goons get the idea. They scream and holler as they tear the furniture apart. Glee on their faces. Mark and Michelle storm away from their safe place. Join in. It's the first time in a long time that any of em have felt anything beyond terror.

The *hate* is still there, though.

Cuz it has to be.

They pile kindling at the bases of the bookshelves with laughing jars. All this cracked dry wood and fabric.

The goons move the body of their fallen comrade to the pyre. "Adios, brother."

They back away. Make room for Athena and her fire.

She touches her torch to the tinder.

The blaze catches on fast. Wood ignites in a flash. Vents in the ceiling suck away most of the smoke.

The music stops.

For the first time since she got here, Athena hears no nothing over the speakers. Just the crackling of flames. The *woosh* as the fire spreads. Engulfs the bookcases and the jars filled with laughing faces.

Then instead of listening to the wood burn, they hear the green liquid in the jars boil.

Laughs become screams. The faces in the jars don't smile anymore. They shriek and wail. They gnash their teeth as they cook.

The six survivors of Frankie's insanity grin.

Enjoy the sights while Frankie's world burns around em.

Athena's happy to think that she's pissed him off so much the ratfuck can't even muster the words to yell over the speakers.

# 17.

There are three doors in Frankie's living room. Ready to be opened and explored amid the smoke.

Athena decides to go clockwise and nobody in the group has the standing to disagree.

Left. Forward. Then right.

She pushes open the first door—the left door—with the barrel of her .45. She steps onto polished metal like stainless steel. Might be. Probably is. Only wonder is that it ain't chrome.

Nobody points out that she's wobbling on her feet.

And she sure as shit doesn't point out that her vision's kinda fucked from blood loss.

The hallway ahead is long and narrow. There are buttons on the wall to the left and right. But nobody knows what hell they might unleash, so they remain untouched.

Athena creeps ahead. Slow. Cautious.

She peeks around the corner where the hallway opens into the room proper. Blinks. Sees examination tables. Five. Sheets over the lumps that lie on em. Blood stains fresh enough they haven't turned brown yet.

Mark takes the lead.

This place looks almost like a hospital. So it's at least close to his wheelhouse.

He approaches the nearest stainless steel table. Prods the bloodied sheet and the lump with the tip of his spear. When it doesn't freak out and try to kill him, he pushes the mess over. It hits the floor with a wet smack.

There are notes scattered around. Hand-drawn diagrams of surgeries. Proposed and completed. One wall has a backlit board for x-rays. A few dozen of em. Black plastic held up by magnets that shows white-blue bones put together in all kinds of fucked up ways. Hands with eyeballs. Humans with lamprey for heads. Cat-dogs.

If the industrial area was for the creation of combat machinery, this's where Frankie made his flesh-bound freaks. Regardless of how...personal Frankie got with his work, there are robotic arms at the head of every table. And shutters in the wall. Computer terminals below the shutters.

Athena lifts one. Peers down the dark stretch.

It's a conveyor belt. The manufactory is on the other damn side.

Mark taps the stainless steel surgical table. Nods to Athena. "Hop up. I gotta do something about that wound on your leg or you aren't going anywhere."

The words ARTERIES. VEINS. SEVERED. BLEED OUT.

They all pop up in Athena's mind.

She doesn't wanna die here.

She *refuses* to die here.

She tries to jump up onto the operating table. Fails the first time. Stops. Catches her breath. Inhales big. Grinds her teeth and sets her jaw. Eyes down.

Athena tries to hop up again.

Fails.

Furrows her brow.

She growls. Pissed off.

Michelle waddles to the other side of the table. Offers her hand.

Athena slaps her away.

Tries again.

Fails again.

Then her knees start to give out.

They jiggle. Wobble from side to side.

Mark catches her.

Goons run forward to help.

They lift her onto the table.

«C'mon Hellcat.»

Athena sneers. Frowns. "F-fuck you all."

She fights against everyone. Everything.

Locks a hand around Mark's throat.

Till Mark puts a palm to her chest and shakes his head. "I don't think I can save the leg."

Then Athena stops. And she's heartbroken. Soulcrushed. And she doesn't have the strength to fight anyone away anyway.

So she pulls her 1911 and puts it to her head.

Mark grabs it. Wraps his hand around her and the gun. "Doesn't mean you're dead." He grabs Athena's jaw. Forces her to look at him. He snaps his fingers in front of her face. "Stay with me." Casts his eyes to the machinery around him. "I have an idea."

Athena drops her gun. Snatches at him with weak hands. "I'd rather be dead. Don't you fuckin dare."

Mark's lips become a hard line. "Unfortunately for you, you're the best hope I have of getting my sister out of here."

Athena wants to say "Fuck you."

Tries very hard to say "Fuck you."

But Mark presses a button on the table.

And everything goes dark.

# 18.

You can live a month in every second of a dream. Fuck the movie bullshit. It's just a fact of our subconscious minds.

Which nobody quite understood.

And there's probably nobody alive to figure out anymore.

So Athena dreams.

Dreams for years.

Dreams about her life before the germ hit.

When she was a gearhead working as a bartender at some shitkicker suckhole in Manhattan called THE THING. Cuz she lost her teaching gig for boozing and it was a question of crawling back to her family's business at the auto shop or striking out on her own.

So fuck it.

They weren't wrong to can her. If you'd put a match to Athena's breath, she'd've started a forest fire.

So she went out on her own.

She'd rather do her time her own way than listen to anyone telling her she had to do *anything* the "right way."

Bartending ain't that bad. Not even as a woman.

There're the pervs and the weirdos. Sure.

But if you're strong and don't take shit, well... Let's just say they like the idea of a challenge and tip even better if they're being kicked in the metaphysical balls.

There's a strange idea about "taming" women that exists in the barfly culture.

Mix tattoos with blonde, the woman's suddenly exotic.

It becomes the goal of the barfly to "tame" the bartender in some capacity.

Which never worked, but Athena enjoyed the tips.

At least until David wandered in one day.

David.

White. Average height. Brown hair. Blue eyes. Kinda guy who wasn't super fit but didn't hurt your vision too much either. Always wore jeans and flannel.

A gearhead himself who got Athena to talking.

Then got Athena to dating.

And they enjoyed making fun of dumb movies. Enjoyed smoking and drinking and bullshitting. And she didn't have a problem moving to Jersey if that meant they could live together and work on cars together.

Then came the cancer.

His in his lungs.

Hers along her skin.

They got closer after that. More like a single organism than anything.

United in disease.

They woke up. In each other's arms. And for some reason, there were a fuckload fewer people on the road. It wasn't even that their cars had crashed. No wrecks.

People just...*weren't there anymore.*

A fine fact of life for Athena and David.

Just smoke. Drink. Eat. Fuck. Raid.

Athena got pregnant. Felt it. Knew it.

CVS test proved it.

Stress and strain made her lose it.

Natural abortion.

Miscarriage.

And they held each other. Consoled each other.

Doesn't matter very much.

But that's what Athena dreams of.

# 19.

Athena's eyes snap open.

She rotates on her ass and hops off the surgical table. Gun in hand.

Mutters to herself, "The fuck just happened."

She hops off the stainless steel she was asleep on. Sees all the congealed blood. Steps away from it.

Takes a moment.

Remembers she's in Frankie's house.

Frankie's surgical bay.

Right. Sure.

She remembers that.

Good first step.

Mark saying...some shit about how he had an idea.

An idea about what?

The guy finally gets authoritative and it's lost on her.

Pieces fall together.

She struts outta the surgery area.

Wait.

Struts?

She lights a cigarette. Leans against the wall.

Goes over all that crap.

Eviscerators. Cyclops fuckers. Thigh ruined.

So...

Athena shakes her head. "No."

Reaches down past the black pig-nosed boot on her right leg. Rolls the leather of her pants up. Inch by inch.

She sees a glint.

A hint.

Shakes her head. "*No*."

She barges out the door of the medical lab. Back into the charred remains of Frankie's living room. Doesn't see any goons. Only sees Mark and Michelle huddled together as usual in a corner. They've dragged an ancient sofa there.

Mark spots her. Shrieks, "Wait, wait."

Athena grabs him by his collar. "What the fuck did you do to me?"

Mark holds his hands up. Submissive. "You would have died. Lost the leg anyway. The veins and arteries weren't just cut, they were *crushed*. Ruined."

"What. The fuck. Did you do to me."

"I saved you."

Michelle reaches a hand toward Athena. "You don't realize how bad off you were."

Athena smacks Michelle's hand away again. "Suck my dick." She sniffs. Casts her eyes around the room. Sees no goons at all. Says, "Where are the others?"

Mark shifts in his spot. "They wanted to keep looking while you were under anesthesia."

Michelle stares at the far door near the fireplace. Her voice like a scared child. "Something came out of the door and took them."

Athena blinks at her. "Something?"

Mark nods. "A crab...spider...thing"

Michelle stares at the floor. "It reached a claw out. Snapped the first guy in two."

"He fell apart at the spine. Upper body flopped down to meet his boots."

"But he was still...tethered together by neural tissue. Screaming."

"The other two tried to fight. But Mister Snips got them too."

Athena cocks an eye. "'Mister Snips?'"

Mark flaps a hand. "The crab thing. It dragged the bodies away."

Athena sets her jaw. Looks around. Bites her lip. "What'd *you* guys do?"

"We, uh..." Mark spreads his hands. "Ran back here."

"Back into the dust, where it's safe." Athena nods. Voice rising to give emphasis to her anger. "Where it's safe, sure. I coulda been torn to ribbons under anesthesia I didn't agree to. And you *watched* fighters stronger than you get taken apart." She grabs a magazine— *Golf Digest*, which seems to inhabit every doctor's office ever, but nobody wants to read it. She curls it up in her hands and slaps Mark with it.

He flinches.

She smacks him like a dog that's shitted the floor. Drops the magazine. Delivers a heavy open-palm slap to Michelle's face. One that rings out the same as a flank steak tossed against the ground. Cuz Michelle's disappointed Athena the most.

Athena spits. "You *cowards*. Those Iron Cross assholes may not have been worth much out there—" she juts her chin toward the wall. "But they were fighters." She stands back. Checks the mag on her 1911. "They tried, at least. You ran."

Mark squints at Athena. Stands. Gets in her face. "Hey, how's being alive treating you? You like being alive? You like not bleeding to death? You like being able to *walk*?"

He throws his hands out. Waits for some retort from Athena. She has none.

He says, "Yeah. Well, you're welcome."

Silence settles between em.

Frankie pipes up on the speakers. "Find me, Mommy."

Athena pops a cigarette between her lips. Groans. "I just want my fuckin car." Lights it. She turns her head. Looks to the door near the fireplace then the one on the right wall. "Which door did—" She cocks her head. Shuts her eyes for a second. "Which door did 'Mister Snips' pop out from?"

Mark points. "Door on the right wall."

Athena nods. Walks toward the door near the fireplace instead. Unslings her sawed-off shotgun. Holds it at the ready.

She taps the door handle.

Throws it open.

Finds hardwood floor under her feet.

Finds...a very nice art deco study.

Athena cracks her neck. Stares.

Whole room is just a ten by ten space with a desk. More bookshelves. Brown armchair.

Mark flicks his fingers from book title to book title. Reads em aloud. "*Book of Azathoth. Eibon. Iod. Cthaat Aquadingen. De Vermis Mysteriis. Hroza Libre. Liber Ivonis. Necronomicon. Pnakotic Manuscripts. Unaussprechlichen Kulten.*"

Athena moves toward Frankie's desk. "Okay."

"I don't know." Mark watches Athena. "The guy is very, very heavily invested in occult teachings. That's all I can say."

Athena pushes the chair behind the desk with a few fingers. Her gun still up. She rolls it back to see if there's some trap door under it.

There ain't.

So she grabs it and sits in it and rifles through Frankie's drawers.

Tells Mark, "None of that means anything to me." She looks to him. "Other than the obvious: which's that he's pants-on-head insane."

Mark keeps on his quest to study Frankie's personal Library. Hits a row of books. "And then there's Lovecraft."

Athena shakes her head. "So?"

Mark swallows. Stares at Athena. "If you actually pay attention to what Frankie's been doing..." Mark rubs his forehead. "He's a *child.* Okay? A wrecked human operating off occult bullshit and the early twentieth century writings of HP Lovecraft.»

Athena sniffs. Lights a cigarette. "I have no idea what any of that *means*."

Mark pleads with her. Puts his hands out. Palm up. "It's all about cosmic horror. A belief that all gods are ancient aliens. Powerful motherfuckers. And to know them is insanity. To even glimpse them is insanity. Because we can *never ever* actually know the universal truths."

Athena squints. "But Frankie thinks he 'knows' em."

"Yeah." Mark crosses his arms. "The weirder point is that none of these books deal with ending the world. Not quite. They treat the end of the world as an inevitability. Like our planet was a thing always meant to be offered up..." He shakes his head. "Harvested for something greater."

She pulls open another drawer. Finds notebook atop notebook. Thesis papers, she thinks. Digs deeper.

Finds photos at the bottom of em all. Arches her eyebrows. Mutters, "Christ."

She slaps the pictures onto the top of the desk. So Mark and Michelle can see.

And there in the Kodak snaps are a young blond boy and his mother—who Athena's a dead goddamn ringer for.

In the photo, it's little pre-crazy Frankie. Looks like he's around ten. He holds a sheet of paper as big as his chest. If Athena squints, she can make out three pieces of writing: MIT. YOUNG INNOVATOR.

Athena leans her head back.

She recites her mantra in her mind:

*I am strong. I am death. I am the absence of forgiveness. There is no poetry for me, for I am that. Strength. Death. The absence of forgiveness.*

# 20.

Athena topples the bookcases. Empties the drawers from Frankie's desk. Piles his notes and sketches. Tosses that damn photo of him as a young boy with his blonde-haired mother on top.

She torches it all.

Storms out to the main room and its ashes.

Final fuckin door.

Athena motions for Mark and Michelle to stand back.

Michelle clutches her pike. Whispers, „Mister Snips."

Frankie's voice creeps over the speakers again. "Are you sure you want to go down there, Mommy?" He titters. "It's very unpleasant."

Athena keeps her shotgun up. Throws the door open. Jumps back.

No Mister Snips. But there's a helluva stench. A fetid odor. A mix of decayed meat and mildew.

She has to cover her nose.

As for what's down that hall, she can't tell. It's too dark. There's a faint light in the distance. A hundred feet or so.

Athena snaps her fingers at Mark. "Find a flashlight."

Mark cocks his head. "Where am I going to find a flashlight? We've burned everything in here."

"Fuckin surgical area, I dunno." She listens. Thinks she can hear something wet in the hallway. Drips and splashes. "Just find me a light."

Mark groans and sets off.

Michelle walks to Athena's side. Waves her hand in front of her nose. "God, that smell..."

Athena grunts.

Michelle waits and listens. "What the hell is in there?"

"Wish I knew."

Mark returns with a pen light. It's kinda shitty, but it'll do.

Athena clicks it on. Casts it down the hallway.

She sees the source of the stink and the sloshing.

The whole corridor is constructed from muscle and metal. Meat that lives and pulses along with some unseen heart that beats in the darkness. The muscle drips blood between ridges of sculpted chrome bones. The floor shudders and sighs. The ceiling droops.

Michelle shakes her head. "I'm not going in there."

Athena wanders away. Grabs some splintered wood. Makes another torch. Sparks it up. Its yellow glow is even weaker than the shitty pen light, but that's not what she's got it for.

She moves the torch into the hall. Just passed the doorframe. Then tosses it in.

The fire hisses and sputters against the damp flesh floor.

The muscle jerks away. Tries to retreat from the flames. A mouth opens farther down along the wall. It screams. Full-throated pain and gives way to rage.

Athena takes aim with her shotgun. Pulls both triggers.

Buckshot slams into the mouth's lips. Punctures em. Cracks teeth. Bloodies the tongue.

The scream gives way to gurgles.

Athena reloads. Slams two fresh shells home. Fires again.

Another haze of pellets shuts the mouth up.

Athena takes a tentative step onto the meat. Tests it. Soft but firm. Like walking on that spongy crap they added to playgrounds to protect children from themselves.

She looks back to Mark and Michelle. "You guys make some more torches. I'll watch the hall."

Michelle says, "Watch it for what?"

There's a flash of movement at the far end.

Athena senses it before she sees it.

A pale skinny hairless humanoid that gallops on all fours. It takes quick, ragged breaths as it runs. That's the only sound in the air right now. Concentrated panting. Phlegmy air-sucking.

The pale thing jumps from the floor to the wall. Clings to the striated muscle there. Takes big fistfuls in its grip. It waits inside the glow from the dying torch. The monster's eyeless. A head that's almost a perfect sphere with a slit of a mouth. But no damn eyes or nose.

The blind freak sniffs the air. Clicks together needle-shaped teeth.

When it gets a bead on Athena, it drops.

Gallops toward her. Snarls.

She redecorates its face with buckshot at close range. The pellets tear away all the skin. Fracture the spherical skull. Send giblets of brain splashing down to the pulsing flesh floor.

Michelle waddles off to make torches.

Three more pale gallopers attack in the meantime. And Athena shatters their faces again. The key problem with that is it leaves her with only four shells for the shotgun. Two barrels and one reload.

Not so good.

But she's got a mag in her 1911 and four spares in pouches on her lower back. Thirty-five rounds for her .45.

If her aim is true, she can probably knock the head off any more gallopers that threaten once the shotgun becomes useless.

Athena moves forward. Shotgun in her right hand. Pen light up in her left.

The flesh floor under her heaves and sighs.

Mark and Michelle stay as close as they can. Guided only by Athena's light. Her occasional puff on a cigarette.

The three *squish squish* along. Footsteps in the mud of bloody muscle under em.

An eye opens above in the ceiling. So bright and blue. It blinks.

Athena puts her cigarette out in it.

The tunnel convulses.

The eye cries. Delicate tears fall. Land on the bleeding muscle. Create clear puddles.

It dawns on Athena that this...is some kind of dirty birth canal for Frankie. On one side is the world where he's the boss. On the other wise is whatever womb he's made for himself.

And she hates it.

And Frankie's probably watching em through those tears.

So she wastes two shotgun shells and blasts the ocular abomination.

The floor convulses again. Seizes.

Thick jelly explodes down.

Athena cracks open the shotgun. Drops the spent shells. Reloads.

They come to a T-junction where the light is. A bulb encased inside metal bars amid the meat. To the left and right is more flesh interwoven with chrome bones. Tunnels with hints of lights at the end.

There's no way to know the correct path.

Athena sucks her teeth. Weighs her options.

A galloper rounds the corner. Jumps to the wall. Sniffs.

She ruins its face. The creature drops with a bloody slap.

Athena dumps her shotgun. Heads toward the corpse.

Mark hisses. "Wait, wait. How do you know that's the right way?"

Athena shrugs. "It's to the right." She pulls her .45. "C'mon." Athena grabs the torch in Mark's hand. Chucks it into the darkness.

The muscle tries to recede again. Can't. Doesn't scream this time but some small mouth squeals. Once. Quick. Then it's quiet again.

No more gallopers. And still no Mister Snips. But Athena keeps her 1911 and pen light up. She wants to move ahead. Get outta the flesh tunnels. It ain't quite that she's scared. Or creeped out.

Just sucks in here.

And it's weird.

And she wonders why they're having such an easy time.

Maybe Frankie never thought anyone would ever make it this far. Given all he's done, it should've been easy enough to create trapdoors. Catch an interloper unaware. Send em screaming down into a new pit and a new nightmare.

On the other hand, a lotta what Frankie did was half-assed with no planning involved. His core strength was mostly in being a fuckin loon.

Athena doesn't even know if his "research" into cancer and children went any farther than torture. Psychological and physical.

She intends to keep her promise to him, though.

She will kill him.

Get the Hellcat.

Get gone from...wherever they are.

Athena thinks about Bullhorn for a moment. She could use someone like that. A co-pilot to help get through the heartland and the western coast. Guy'd be a shitload more of a combat boost in the wastes than Mark or Michelle.

If he's alive, anyway.

She shakes her head.

David flashes through her mind.

Ah, fuck.

The meat tunnel turns to the left. Then they find themselves at another junction. Straight ahead or right. The path to the right terminates at an alarmingly labial curtain of meat. Straight ahead looks like it loops around to the left. Back to where they were.

Sad fucker Frankie still half-assing it. Working in obvious lines.

Athena votes vagina.

The three of em turn to the right. Approach the meat curtain.

Michelle drops her torch. Holds both hands around the pike.

Mark does the same.

Athena pushes through.

The meat curtains are a soaking mess of blood and some clear drool. It stains Athena's head. The little blonde hair there. Her leather.

Mark gets more. His already dirty white and black plaid shirt comes through as though it's been dragged through an abattoir.

Michelle is dead-eyed. Her torn blue jeans and ragged hoodie suck up the blood. So her clothes are fat and warped with the fluids.

They emerge out the other side into a room that's carpeted light blue. Wall-papered to looks like a sky with fluffy white clouds.

The blood from their boots leaves vicious red footprints.

The room is small and comparatively less gaudy than the rest of Frankie's funhouse.

To the left is a kitchen with black and white tile. An old sink. Counter. Fridge. Oven.

To the right is a small living room. Couch. Lounger. Bulky television with antennae. A bookcase. Then not even a door. Just a *poster* of a door.

Athena thinks it looks like some bygone TV set. If there was room behind em for the audience, she'd be spot on.

Mark says, "This is some weird 'Leave it to Beaver' shit."

She doesn't disagree. Her lips become a thin bloodless line.

There's a door beyond the kitchen. A note stapled to it that reads: "FRANKIE'S PLACE | KEEP OUT" and a smiley face. All drawn in multiple colors of Crayola.

Athena keeps his pistol barrel down. Marches. The gun tight in her grip. She runs a gloved hand across her forehead. Her short hair. Flecks the hemoglobin off like sweat. She tucks up on the left side of the door. Ready to breach.

She nods to Mark.

He nods back. Hunches up on the right. Pike held tight. Waits for either the door to open or for her to signal.

Michelle keeps her distance.

With good reason.

Athena takes a breath. Stares at the floor. Inhales. Exhales.

Knocks on the door.

Once. Twice.

Frankie's voice pipes up. "Moooooom. I'm busy."

Athena tilts her head. Licks her lips. Her eyes bounce from Mark's to Michelle's. She swallows. Breathes again. Asks Frankie, "Busy with what, dear?"

A hushed silence. The sounds of hurried movement. "Nothing!"

As though this's nothing more harmful than a mother interrupting a pud-pull session.

Athena pounds the door with her left hand. "*Frankie*. What're you doing in there?"

"Nothing! Why won't you leave me alone? You said you would once dad died." His voice in hysterics. "You promised you'd let me study." Frankie huffs and puffs. "You knew how important his research was. He tried to teach me but you wouldn't *leave us alone*."

Athena grimaces. "Fuck this."

She fires twice into the door's lock. Shatters the metal there.

Storms in.

Has five bullets for Frankie.

Finds Frankie strung up by hooks in his back and nipples.

The dipshit floats at the foot of his rocket ship-shaped bed. Suspended by wires and a contraption she doesn't even know what to do with.

There are candles in an offset pentagram below his feet.

He's naked. Wearing a black robe and nothing else. Dick and balls dangle.

Athena trains her pistol on him. Cocks an eyebrow. "You're... Is this a ritual kinda thing?"

Frankie smiles. "I understand them, Mommy. I can talk to them and they can talk to me. I can bring them here. The dark gods. The ones who have waited all this time between the rolling black spheres. Gravitational—"

"Holy shit. I don't care."

Frankie smiles. "*Me detraham tenebrarum. Adducam e nigris here. Qui tam multa sciant. Nunc per exsilia—*"

Athena puts a .45 round through Frankie's elephant cock. Then fires another.

The mad doctor's fat member drops with a wet slap. Whatever balls he had ain't there anymore. The new ragged hole in his body pisses blood.

He screams and spins on his strings. The hooks through his nipples rip and tear as he shrieks.

Athena sits on the edge of his bed. Notices brown cookie crumbs on the sheets. "There's nothing out there for you, Frankie." She rifles through his bedside drawers till she finds his remote control. "Now." She squints at him. Wiggles the remote. "Where's my fuckin car?"

Frankie groans. Pants. Mewls. "I loved that penis." He sniffs. Says, "Garage."

"Where's the garage, Frankie?"

"It's out....siiiiide." He eyes grow sad and dead. "The garage number is fifty-seven fifty-seven."

"Where are the main doors and how do I open em?"

Frankie sighs. "You hit 'four four six five' in the theater."

"And the code for door to get back to the mess hall?"

"Nine six nine eight."

Athena stands. "Now, as sad as this is for you? Your world tumbling down?" She caresses Frankie's sweaty face. "It gets worse." She wraps her fingers between the strands of his damp hair. Pulls on it. "I'm gonna watch while Mark and Michelle work you over."

The brother and sister don't smile. They stare at Frankie. Eyes a little glassy. Lips dead set in lines.

To Athena, they look like animals.

Hungry animals whose dinner is here dangling on meat hooks. About fuckin time they got in line with her.

Frankie must recognize the look too. He kicks in the air. His legs hit nothing. "What do you mean?" He kicks again. Struggles. "The dark ones didn't come for me. They didn't come." He starts to cry. "Why didn't they come, Mommy? That was what all of this was for..."

Athena smiles. "Cuz the crap about old gods and *any* gods is total bullshit." Athena caresses Frankie's face. "Nothing and nobody is looking out for you." She steps back. Nods to Mark and Michelle. Locks her eyes on Frankie. "You got a debt needs paying." She smirks. "Makes you feel any better, *Mommy* gets to put you outta you're misery."

Frankie smiles. "But maybe the old gods will come for you."

\* \* \*

Mark and Michelle run Frankie through every perversity they can muster.

They slide their pikes down his throat till he pukes. Up his ass till his intestines can't look like much more than red and brown scrambled eggs.

The stench of bodily fluids amassing under Frankie's body is only mitigated by Athena's chain smoking.

And she can't help but wonder how much of the shit Mark and Michelle are doing to Frankie now is from what he pulled on em in the labs.

Michelle finds a pair of scissors in his bedside dresser. She twists and the arms snap apart. She hands one blade to Mark. Keeps the other for herself.

They take turns slashing at him. Hacking little bits of him away.

Mark glides the sharp edge against Frankie's nipples. The flesh starts to come away. Pulled taught by gravity and the hooks. Then both pink parts of Frankie are ripped off.

He eventually stops crying. Maybe shock takes hold.

The two have their cathartic fun till Athena gets bored of his shrieks.

Says, "Enough."

She grabs Frankie by his hair. Tilts his head so she talks right into his ear. "I know I'm going to hell. I want you to wait for me there."

He blinks. A dumb creature.

Mark and Michelle managed to break him.

She puts a .45 slug through his head.

Michelle frowns.

Mark grunts.

Like they both wanted some more time with the demented motherfucker.

# 21.

Mark and Michelle don't talk much after that. Like Athena, they grunt or shrug unless they really *need* to open their mouths.

The trio exits Frankie's birth canal. Make their way to the hall that should lead to the cafeteria. Except for the big metal door.

Athena holds up the remote. Looks over the buttons. There's the keypad—one through nine and a zero at the bottom like on a mobile phone—plus a star and a pound sign at the bottom. A green key and a red key at the top.

Seems like Frankie just ripped it from some cheapo flip phone.

Which doesn't matter, but it's got her curious about all the buttons and the combinations of buttons.

If she hits six six six, does this facility sink into the abyss?

Would sixty-nine launch any remaining creatures on a sexual adventure?

Athena squints. She doesn't even know if there's another floor to this place. Maybe something above or below. More mysteries and weirdness.

Well, fuck it and fuck that.

She punches in nine six nine eight. Hits the green button.

The big metal door to the cafeteria groans. Recedes up into the ceiling.

Carnage waits on the other side. All the blood and bodies from the fight that was...an hour ago? Two?

Time goes sideways under stress and combat.

The new item in the wreckage is an Eviscerator. The machine slumped over. As though it's a bit drunk and needs a wall to lean on till it feels better.

There's no body in it. No Sherlock or Bullhorn. No sign of the other powered armor either.

Plenty of dents from high-caliber bullets in the walls though. Scorch marks too.

Okay.

Great.

The trio heads left. Toward the theater. And supposedly the doors that lead outside.

Athena stands at the top of the stairs. Looks down at the stage.

She thinks of Frankie's little show. The insanity and abuse after. She sneers at the memory of it. Lifts the remote. Taps four four six five.

Bullhorn's voice booms down the hall. From the direction of Frankie's machine shop. "Hellcat?"

Athena sees his silhouette rush their way. There's something rectangular in his hand and he's flanked by someone she assumes is Sherlock. She shouts, "I'm getting us outta here."

Bullhorn's red-lit body skids to a halt. He puts his arm up and stops Sherlock. He says, "You got Frankie's remote?"

She nods. Holds it up. Presses the green key.

Bullhorn shouts. "Fuckin *don't*."

Athena squints at him.

He holds up the book thing in his hand. It's a tablet. He clicks a button and his face is lit by a white glare. "Sherlock pulled the schematics and the remote codes from Frankie's computer." He shakes the tablet. "That ain't the way out."

Athena cocks an eyebrow.

Bullhorn stays where he is. Won't go any farther. "It's his goddamn aquarium."

Athena blinks.

Ah, shit.

Alarms blare. The far theater wall slides apart. Thirty feet tall. Fifty feet wide. In an agonizing and slow process.

Blue light cascades in against the red. The wall gives way to a massive curvature of glass. Thousands of gallons of lapping water behind it.

Athena sees dark shapes in the water. Some are long, slender things. They float at about middle height in the tank. Others are closer to the bottom. Fat saucers with claws. A whole collection of Mister Snipses. Ain't anything up at the top.

But the water gets darker.

And darker.

The shadow of something pushing itself forward.

It blocks out the light from the tank. Slams against the glass. The weight and force of the beast create a spider web of cracks.

Tentacles. Dozens of limbs with pink suckers affix themselves to the side of the aquarium. A nightmare combination of octopus and lizard. Octopus for a head and face. Dragon for a body. Except several hundred times bigger than it should be.

Sherlock grabs the tablet from Bullhorn. Shouts, "Subject #1937."

Bullhorn shouts after him. "We should *leave*."

Subject #1937 presses against the glass. One of the big silvery hubcap eyes on its head stares down. It's clawed fingers scratch.

Athena gawks at its massiveness. This kraken.

And the thing gawks back.

There's a hint of recognition in that eye.

Like it *knows* Athena ain't Frankie.

And maybe it's kinda pissed about that.

She imagines the kraken saying, *"Who's this bitch?"* And backs away.

Mark stares. He watches the titanic writhing, pulsing monstrosity. "Frankie wanted the dark ones to be with him so badly that he created one." Mark offers the air a sad chuckle. "He made a Cthulhu."

Athena maintains her backward gait.

Michelle grabs Mark's shoulder. Tugs her brother.

The trio marches in the direction of away.

Bullhorn waves em on.

The kraken watches. Cries out. Its voice a sad whale song. The pitch stretches from innards-shaking deep to ear-piercing high.

It slams against the side of the aquarium.

More cracks appear along the glass.

Athena, Mark and Michelle run to Bullhorn and Sherlock.

The trio becomes five.

They jump over bodies. Happy their boots have enough traction to keep em from slipping in the blood. From slipping and whacking their heads against one of the goddamn picnic tables.

Glass shatters.

Liquid spills.

They hear the rush of a sudden and unrelenting and violent tsunami.

Bullhorn leads em around one of the far corners in Frankie's manufactory.

It puts em in yet another big hallway. One with conveyors that churn up from the guts of industry. One designed to move the bone machines out to the world. Where they can wreak their havoc. Retrieve bodies and machines for Frankie.

Bullhorn pounds the two titanic doors that stretch far, far above his head.

The kraken calls.

Sherlock taps his tablet in frantic movements. "Code for the outer door is—"

Athena watches a thin rivulet of water slide across the surface of the metal flooring. It touches her boot. She moves back. 1911 in her right hand. Remote in her left.

"—Fuck, it's just one. Just hit *one*."

Athena does. Clicks the green button.

The tall metal gate behind em squeals. Pulls itself apart.

Athena watches the slit spread.

Mark and Michelle push their backs against it.

The tip of a blue tentacle curls around the wall.

Athena puts two .45 rounds in it.

The kraken cries. Pulls back.

Water floods the floor.

They all stand in pools of fetid aquarium funk.

Michelle throws herself through the opening. Out into the world.

Mark follows.

Then Sherlock.

Bullhorn shoves Athena through. Tumbles out after her.

They land on pavement. In the cool night air. Surrounded by blue streetlights.

They back away and run from the screaming kraken that wants to be out and causing chaos.

Athena hits one on the remote. Stabs the green button with her thumb again.

The big metal doors reverse their course. Start to come together.

One of the kraken's tentacles lashes out. Streams high up into the night sky and slams down on the asphalt. The only thing its suckers retrieve is broken pieces of blacktop.

The doors continue their slow shuttering.

The tentacle gets stuck.

The hydraulics of the gate whine. Struggle. Press into the blue flesh of the kraken. Till the skin reaches its pressure point and ruptures.

Frankie's prison craps out a twenty foot piece of Subject #1937.

The kraken inside howls. It throws itself against the sliding heavy metal doors. They jump on their tracks. But they hold.

Athena lights a cigarette.

Watches the chunk of tentacle wriggle. Die. Deflate.

She glances toward a squat grey disconnected building she figures is the garage. It's a safe distance from Frankie's. Maybe in case someone planted a bomb in their ride to get him.

It's the temporary home of her Hellcat. Athena can't wait to get back into the driver's seat, but there's something else she needs to see first.

Her boot stomps are loud in the stillness of the night. Loud as she storms away from Frankie's and over to a dusty hillock next to a dusty field for a better look at where the fuck she's been held for the duration of this bullshit.

She looks back at Frankie's place. Tall and chrome—it reflects everything. A mirror laid out like a Byzantine cross, she knows now. Just the one big floor. Nothing above. But maybe something below.

Beyond that are two fat pregnant stacks in the distance. Sloped. Grey in the lights from Frankie's compound. Mushrooms without the caps. Two titans that stand tall as the sun's rays bounce against their eastern sides.

Athena pulls a face like someone farted.

Bullhorn approaches her and nods toward her cigarette.

She hands him a stogie.

He sits in the dust.

She lights his American Spirit.

He takes a drag. Blows smoke. "Welcome to the Perry nuclear plant." He takes another pull. "All the wonders of the nuclear age slapped up against Lake Erie." Bullhorn looks up toward Athena.

She says, "I thought these all went down."

Bullhorn shrugs. "Most did. Perry failed-safe. Frankie... Frankie probably had a mom who worked at the plant. Maybe a dad and—"

"I don't give a shit who Frankie was. We know *what* he was."

Bullhorn blinks. "Yeah." He tucks his feet under him in the dust. Shifts into a cross-legged position. "Yeah, fuck it."

The two stand and sit and watch the sun come up. Orange rays of light against industry and their own personal smoke stacks between their fingers.

Old money dissolved to dust.

Industry decayed.

Athena looks back. Finds Sherlock.

The kid chatting in panicked relief with Mark and Michelle.

He smiles at her.

She reminds herself that this whole load of fuckers was trying to kill her a few days before. "What's the code to shut this place down for good."

Sherlock tilts his head. "I don't—"

"Frankie wasn't a stupid lunatic. The *Iron Cross* is filled with stupid lunatics." Athena sniffs. "He wouldn't want anyone touching his research." She narrows her eyes. "*I* sure as shit don't want anyone touching his research."

"You mean you wanna blow it all up."

Athena nods.

Mark and Michelle trudge up behind Sherlock.

Sherlock looks to Bullhorn.

Bullhorn shakes his head. Shrugs.

Sherlock takes a deep breath. Licks his lips. "You can probably guess it."

Athena grinds her teeth without thinking. "Six six six."

She enters the numbers on the remote.

Sherlock nods. Backs away. Turns to look at Frankie's big facility. "We could learn something from him. Maybe." Sherlock winces. "Something about the cancer. The bug. Maybe all that madness did lead to a cure. I mean, really, this is a treasure trove of technology. I've never even *heard* of anything like this. Never dreamed of it. If you destroy it, it'll be gone forever." He sighs. "Humanity could use it to get back on its feet. You should *think* about this before you nuke it!"

Athena grunts. Hits the green button.

There's a boom like thunder deep in the facility's guts. It makes the ground tremor. Makes dirt and dust shake. Secondary explosions follow the first. The sound of a giant stomping nearby. *Thud thud thud thud.*

Blue electricity crackles along the roof. Thin tendrils arc down to the walls.

The chrome and the sparks become so bright they have to shield their eyes.

Center of the cross goes up. The intersection where the cafeteria used to be. A great gout of flame screams into the morning sky. Fire flanked by lightning.

Explosions march along the lengths of the cross. Of Frankie's nightmare factory.

The final blast blows apart those heavy front doors.

Athena glares as the kraken is thrown free.

The great beast struggles. Howls. It pulls itself along on weak, broken limbs. Blood pools around Subject #1937 in massive red lakes.

Tentacles around its head reach out. The big hubcap eyes along the side of its face swivel toward Athena and the others.

Mark lays a firm hand on Michelle's shoulder.

Bullhorn smokes.

Sherlock stares.

The kraken growls. It aches along. Pathetic on the pavement. Forever trying to reach its prey at the hillock.

Till finally death takes it. And it can move no more.

Athena drops her cigarette.

# 22.

Athena rolls up a sliding door to the garage. Blinks against the fluorescent lights that dangle from the ceiling.

She sees the repair bays for all the vehicles Frankie's bone machines turned in.

She sees her matte black Hellcat. Repaired. Perfect in every way.

It sits between random vehicles. Including Bullhorn's old pickup truck. One of the Ford Mustang interceptors the Iron Cross used to chase her down.

There are some odd and rare cars too. Ones she'd like to own.

1967 hardtop Chevy Impala.

1971 Plymouth Hemi Cuda.

1973 XB GT Ford Falcon with a blower through the hood.

The Iron Cross goons rush for Bullhorn's pickup.

Athena runs for her Hellcat.

It's been repaired. Bullet holes removed. Glass replaced.

She casts her eyes around at the stationary robot arms in the bay. Guesses the things were automated. Doesn't have a clue why.

Only the inkling that Frankie probably wanted any vehicles in tip-top shape for his own satisfaction.

Bullhorn finds her eyes from the driver's seat of his pickup.

The curiosity on his face matches her own.

Athena slips behind the wheel of the Hellcat. Digs into her jacket pockets for the keys. Finds em. Starts her machine up.

Watches the gas meter level rise. Full tank.

The engine growls.

She slaps the car into neutral. Lays onto the gas pedal.

The engine roars.

She waits for the RPMs to die down. Pushes the shifter back into park. Lets the car idle.

Bullhorn does the same.

Athena steps out. Right hand over the butt of her 1911. She squints at Bullhorn.

He shakes his head. "No. I told you I was tired." He jerks his head toward Sherlock. The kid in the passenger seat of the Ford pickup, poking through the glove compartment. "We're just *tired*, Hellcat. Gonna find some chunk of land near the lakes. Fish and have ourselves a nice, quiet death. All right?" He pushes his hands into the air. "All right?" He walks to the rollup door in front of his Ford. "Can't promise anything about the rest of the Iron Cross, though."

Athena stares at him. Waits for him to open the door. Get back in his truck with Sherlock. Drive away.

They do.

She sniffs. Cracks her neck. Opens the Hellcat's trunk.

The Easy-Bake Oven is still there. The cookies are gone from their container.

Athena remembers the crumbs on Frankie's bed.

Little bastard.

Eating sweets and desperately attempting to summon evil.

Fuckin idiot.

There are a few bottles of water left. No ammo. No water. No food. No toilet paper.

Athena slams the trunk shut.

Watches Mark crawl into the back seat.

Michelle into the front passenger seat.

Athena rubs her face. Listens to the purr of the Hellcat. Grabs the steering wheel when she's back in the driver's seat.

She rolls outta the garage. Passes the smoking heap of Frankie's facility. The smoking heap of the tentacled titan.

She takes the Hellcat south. Onto the first road she finds.

In the rearview mirror, she sees monstrous creatures breach the water of Lake Erie. Stretch into the sky. Then slam back down.

Athena lights a cigarette. Breathes smoke. She bites her bottom lip. Looks to her right at Michelle. Clears her throat. Says, "You can...check the radio, if you want."

She furrows her brow. Keeps an eye out for signs that'll put em on I-90 west.

Michelle reaches a hesitant hand toward the radio. After a moment of fumbling, she figures it out. Scans across the bands for a signal.

Mark's voice sounds from the backseat. "Where are we going?"

Athena blinks into the rearview. Can't see Mark cuz the guy's laid down. She takes a pull from her American Spirit. "Same place we've always been going." She reminds herself to...be her. "West. We're going out west."

Static becomes a voice on the radio:

. 191 .

"—orning all you road runners. I'm Dapper Don. With any luck you caught my less-awesome brother Dan's show last night." Laughter. "If you didn't, well, that's definitely okay. We aren't going anywhere. In spite of what you heard from Dan, we're fairing all right in Columbus these days. There's the mutie problem, sure, and the bugs, sure, but otherwise it's quiet in our sleepy town. Not a heck of a lot of folks around these parts. Aaaaaaanyway, you're here for the music, aren't you? Here's Muse with 'Apocalypse Please.'"

Athena sucks on her cigarette. Guns the Hellcat.

"We can make Columbus."

The road fades into a grey smudge.

Athena peels onto US-20W. Then OH-2W.

The speedometer swings up from sixty to eighty.

Ninety.

A hundred-ten.

And Athena feels free again.

# ABOUT THE AUTHOR

William Vitka is a writer and journalist with more than ten books under his belt and ten years in the news business. He believes that politicians will be the doom of us all, but at least there's whiskey. His Twitter handle is @vitka and he can be found at facebook. com/VitkaWrites.

# BOOK

# PERMUTED PRESS

### needs **you** to help

## SPREAD (THE) INFECTION

# 14

**Peter Clines**

> "A riveting apocalyptic mystery in the style of LOST."
> —Craig DiLouie, author of *The Infection*

Padlocked doors. Strange light fixtures. Mutant cockroaches.

There are some odd things about Nate's new apartment. Every room in this old brownstone has a mystery. Mysteries that stretch back over a hundred years. Some of them are in plain sight. Some are behind locked doors. And all together these mysteries could mean the end of Nate and his friends.

Or the end of everything…

PERMUTED
PRESS

# THE JOURNAL SERIES
## by Deborah D. Moore

After a major crisis rocks the nation, all supply lines are shut down. In the remote Upper Peninsula of Michigan, the small town of Moose Creek and its residents are devastated when they lose power in the middle of a brutal winter, and must struggle alone with one calamity after another.

*The Journal* series takes the reader head first into the fury that only Mother Nature can dish out.

PERMUTED
PRESS

## Michael Clary
### THE GUARDIAN | THE REGULATORS | BROKEN

When the dead rise up and take over the city, the Government is forced to close off the borders and abandon the remaining survivors. Fortunately for them, a hero is about to be chosen...a Guardian that will rise up from the ashes to fight against the dead. The series continues with Book Four: *Scratch*.

## Emily Goodwin
### CONTAGIOUS | DEATHLY CONTAGIOUS

During the Second Great Depression, twenty-four-year-old Orissa Penwell is forced to drop out of college when she is no longer able to pay for classes. Down on her luck, Orissa doesn't think she can sink any lower. She couldn't be more wrong. A virus breaks out across the country, leaving those that are infected crazed, aggressive and very hungry.

The saga continues in Book Three: *Contagious Chaos* and Book Four: *The Truth is Contagious*.

PERMUTED
PRESS

## THE BREADWINNER | Stevie Kopas

The end of the world is not glamorous. In a matter of days the human race was reduced to nothing more than vicious, flesh hungry creatures. There are no heroes here. Only survivors. The trilogy continues with Book Two: *Haven* and Book Three: *All Good Things.*

## THE BECOMING | Jessica Meigs

As society rapidly crumbles under the hordes of infected, three people—Ethan Bennett, a Memphis police officer; Cade Alton, his best friend and former IDF sharpshooter; and Brandt Evans, a lieutenant in the US Marines—band together against the oncoming crush of death and terror sweeping across the world. The story continues with Book Two: *Ground Zero.*

## THE INFECTION WAR | Craig DiLouie

As the undead awake, a small group of survivors must accept a dangerous mission into the very heart of infection. This edition features two books: *The Infection* and *The Killing Floor.*

## OBJECTS OF WRATH | Sean T. Smith

The border between good and evil has always been bloody... Is humanity doomed? After the bombs rain down, the entire world is an open wound; it is in those bleeding years that William Fox becomes a man. After The Fall, nothing is certain. *Objects of Wrath* is the first book in a saga spanning four generations.

PERMUTED
PRESS